"Jack!"

When his door swung open, Mia couldn't quite stop her headlong rush. She came up against him in the doorway, palms on his chest, body pressed against his. The magazine clattered to the floor.

She couldn't tear her eyes from his. Her heart, already beating too fast, pounded harder. Her breathing sang alongside his, the same sensual song.

His hands had cupped her shoulders, and she could feel the tension in his arms. Was he trying to pull her closer? Or push her farther away? Which did she want?

She tipped her head back, asking for…what? Her conscious self would know and would likely object, but she'd stopped listening to that part of herself. When he lowered his head, she strained up toward him, her fingers curling into his sweater. Her eyes drifted shut and her body opened like a flower to him.

Her knees went weak….

Dear Reader,

I confess, I always fall in love at least a little bit with my heroes. That's never been more true than with Jack Traynor in *Her Miracle Man*. More than once, I wanted to take that man in my arms and give him a great big hug. He became so real to me as the book progressed, I couldn't wait to get to his happily ever after.

As for my heroine, Mia, I couldn't help but feel grateful that she and Jack found each other. Both lost souls in need of protection, they have to travel some bleak landscape to get to the light. But the healing power of love pulls them through.

I hope you enjoy Jack and Mia's journey.

Karen

HER
MIRACLE MAN

KAREN SANDLER

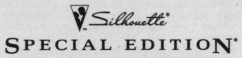

Published by Silhouette Books

America's Publisher of Contemporary Romance

SILHOUETTE BOOKS

ISBN-13: 978-0-373-24901-5
ISBN-10:   0-373-24901-2

HER MIRACLE MAN

Visit Silhouette Books at www.eHarlequin.com

Printed in U.S.A.

Books by Karen Sandler

Silhouette Special Edition

The Boss's Baby Bargain #1488
Counting on a Cowboy #1572
A Father's Sacrifice #1636
His Baby to Love #1686
The Three-Way Miracle #1733
Her Baby's Hero #1751
His Miracle Baby #1890
Her Miracle Man #1901

KAREN SANDLER

first caught the writing bug at age nine when, as a horse-crazy fourth grader, she wrote a poem about a pony named Tony. Many years of hard work later, she sold her first book (and she got that pony—although his name is Ben). She enjoys writing novels, short stories and screenplays and has produced two short films. She lives in Northern California with her husband of twenty-three years and two sons who are busy eating her out of house and home. You can reach Karen at Karen@KarenSandler.net.

To the lost souls of the world
still struggling toward the light.

Chapter One

She was so cold.

The rain had drenched her sweater and jeans and plastered her hair to her head. Chilly rivulets streamed down her face and the back of her neck where they entered her sweater.

She hunched over, pressing against the storm's onslaught. Her eyes were nearly closed as she tried to see where to put her feet. Fallen needles from the surrounding conifers cushioned her steps but concealed ankle-deep puddles, one of which she'd already blundered into. Incense cedars, Ponderosa pines and Douglas firs—she automatically cataloged them as *Calocedrus decurrens, Pinus ponderosa* and *Preudotsuga menziesii*—loomed over her. No doubt wildlife abounded in the surrounding trees and brush, but they all had the sense to hunker down under cover.

She stumbled and nearly went to her knees as the thick

needles suddenly gave way to a gravel road. Thank God there was at least a shred of daylight remaining or she might have traversed the narrow track unknowing. Night would be falling soon. It was nearly… She raised her wrist to check her watch. Gone. Where had she left it?

As if frozen by the icy rain, her mind couldn't muster an answer. Nor could it explain where she was, how she'd gotten here in the first place, why she was wandering these thick woods in an inadequate wool sweater and denim jeans, with only ruined cross-trainers and ankle socks on her feet.

She looked right where the road sloped downhill, then left where it climbed uphill. She could barely make out the sound of running water over the noise of the pounding rain. A creek, maybe.

Downhill seemed safer, more likely to take her back to a main road. But this narrow gravel track must lead somewhere. If she went uphill, she might find a house where she could find shelter.

The cold was dulling her brain, slowing her already-confused thought processes. When the storm miraculously let up for a moment as if it took a slow breath before expending its fury on her again, she peered up the road. In that brief respite she spotted a glimmer of light in the distance.

She turned and started up the gentle slope. The location of that distant light told her that the hill would get steeper as she drew nearer. With barely the energy to put one foot in front of the other, she wasn't sure how she'd find the reserves for a steep climb.

The roar of running water grew louder as she trudged up the road. The storm had regained its muscle, the rain so thick she could hardly breathe. When she reached the creek, she hesitated for a moment, awestruck by the speeding, foaming rush of water cutting across her path. The bridge across it seemed spindly and inconsequential in the face of the creek's power. But she could see the steel girders on either side, the stout metal railing.

From the ruts in the road leading to and away from the bridge, she knew that if the structure could handle a car, it could certainly hold her weight. Exhaustion slowing her, she stepped onto the thick timbers, one hand gripping the rail tightly. This evidence of human development comforted her, gave her an anchor. There were still people in the world. Someone would help her.

She shouldn't have stopped halfway across. But light arcing across the hillside up ahead befuddled her. Her laboring brain seemed to tell her feet to still, so she could work out the source of the light. Just as she looked back, spotting the glare of headlights appearing and disappearing through the trees below, she felt the first wash of water over her feet. Before she could work out why water lapped at her ankles, the creek surged.

The knee-deep wave pulled her feet out from under her. In an instant the flood had swept her under the railing and off the bridge.

Jack Traynor peered through his windshield at the ugly weather, his Suburban creeping along the zigs and zags of his private road. He usually zipped along the five miles of washboard gravel at a bone-jarring clip, the big four-wheel-drive vehicle unfazed by the climb. But when visibility was near zero in a deluge like this, or in a whiteout like the ones that he would no doubt face before December was over, he navigated his sometimes treacherous road more carefully.

When his headlights first brushed the bridge across Sierra

Creek, he thought the rain must be playing tricks with his vision. It looked almost as if someone was on the bridge. But considering the fact that where the creek crossed his sixty acres was a good four miles from Highway 50, that briefly glimpsed silhouette had to be an illusion. Who would walk those four miles in this downpour?

But as Jack drew nearer and drove along a straight stretch that kept his headlights focused on the bridge, he realized the person standing there was no fantasy. How in the hell had they gotten there? He had discouraged hiking with a multitude of Private Property and No Trespassing signs, not that the area surrounding his home was particularly amenable to tourists. Sometimes on balmy summer days he'd have to chase away the odd interloper, but it made no sense that someone would intrude during winter's opening volley.

He supposed it could be a reporter, but not likely. Five years ago they'd been after him like hungry vultures, all of them eager for an exclusive. But now he was old news. Other than the overblown documentary that one of the cable channels aired a year ago, the press ignored him these days.

Keeping his gaze fixed on the woman—at least he'd guessed she was female, based on her slenderness—he goosed the accelerator, increasing his speed as much as he dared. As he got closer, he saw the woman sway and realized that whoever she was and however she'd gotten here, she was in trouble. Instinct told him he'd better get there damn fast.

Not fast enough. Just as he pulled over the last rise, the creek got her, a surge of water upending her. Even as Jack shoved the Suburban into Park and jumped out, he saw her go under. His heart squeezed in a hard, painful knot. He ran toward the bridge, but he knew his effort would be futile. She was dead. There was no way she could survive a ride down this raging creek.

Then he saw the arm hooked around the railing support, the woman struggling to keep her head back and above water. She seemed to squirm from side to side as the creek slammed into her. The water was the least of it. Deadfall in the fast-moving creek could break a bone.

He went in anyway and grabbed her just in time, as her arm grew lax and her head lolled forward in the water. Terrified he'd lose his grip on her, fighting the water's pressure against his lower legs, he clamped his hands under her arms. Battling against the creek's strength, he slid the woman's body back through the railing. He didn't breathe easy until he had her slung over his shoulder in a fireman's carry as he slogged back to his truck.

He set her limp body in the passenger seat, then shucked his heavy duster and spread it over her. A quick check of her carotid revealed a rapid but steady pulse. Her breath curled across his hand when he held it in front of her face.

Slamming the door shut, he rounded the front of the Suburban and got in, soaked to the skin. He cranked the heat up as far as it would go and inched forward. The creek had receded again, although it still spilled a few inches of water over the bridge. Nothing the Suburban couldn't handle. Water fanning off to either side, he sped across as quickly as he dared.

The engine roared as he climbed the last steep segment of his road, windshield wipers barely keeping up with the pounding rain. He'd never been more grateful to pull into the wide asphalt driveway of his log home. Motion sensors above the garage triggered exterior lights, their glow muted by the downpour. He pressed the remote for the garage, then pulled the Suburban inside.

Damn, she was pale, Jack realized as he got his first look at her in the glare of the overhead fluorescents. Her short hair lay slickly against her head. She had red marks across her left cheekbone and a cut above her brow. Both likely caused by the fall from the bridge.

The supplies that had been his reason for heading into town in such lousy weather could wait. The woman was the more pressing concern. Jack carefully lifted her into his arms, the feel of her deadweight sending a chill of fear down his spine. Exactly how his wife had felt the night he'd found her.

Jack blanked that image from his mind, focusing instead on the feel of the woman's breath against his throat where he'd nestled her head. This wasn't Elizabeth he carried into his house. This wasn't the past repeating itself.

He shouldered through the garage door into the dining room, then hurried past to the great room. The lamp he'd left burning in the front window provided enough light to see. Easing the woman into the recliner, he threw sofa cushions onto the floor in front of the fireplace. Thank God for the fast starting pellet stove. It would be kicking out plenty of heat in no time.

He turned back to the woman. If he laid her down on the sofa cushions as she was, those wet clothes would just hold the chill against her skin. He'd have to undress her before he rolled her up in blankets. He doubted she'd like it much when she woke, but she wouldn't die from embarrassment; hypothermia was another matter.

He set aside the duster, then bent to her feet. She'd lost her shoes in the torrent of water so he had only the ankle socks to remove. The gleam of metal around her left ankle caught his eye. He lifted the wet hem of her jeans to reveal a delicate bracelet, the name Mia worked in gold.

Leaving the anklet, Jack unbuttoned the jeans, struggling against the stiff, wet material to lower the zipper. The icy goose-pimpled flesh at the woman's waist urged him to move more quickly. Jeans off, he unpeeled the Christmas-red wool sweater from her upper body.

And he saw the other red marks—along her legs, several just below her rib cage. A nasty scratch, angry crimson but no longer bleeding, marred her left forearm. He checked the sweater, expecting a tear to match the wound, but the left sleeve was intact.

He levered her up, letting her body slump against his. More marks across her back, from shoulder to hip. Seeing them, an old horror crouched inside him, clawed at his belly. Elizabeth, lying on the kitchen floor, her body bruised like this woman's, bloody.

Again he shook the images off. A raging creek could carry with it branches, logs, even rocks. That was what had pounded this woman's body, cut her arm. Rocks and deadfall. Not fists.

Grabbing an afghan from the back of the sofa, he spread it on the cushions. He carefully gathered the woman—Mia?—in his arms and laid her on the afghan. The front of her dusty-pink bra was torn, as if it had caught on something that nearly ripped it off. Maybe a sharp edge on the bridge had snagged it when she went over. He kept his eyes averted as best he could while he pulled away the last barriers to the unconscious woman's modesty, setting the bra and matching panties on the hearth.

He brought the edges of the afghan over the woman, then hurried to the master bedroom for the thick comforter on his bed. Doubling it over, he tucked it around her.

As he stepped back, he shivered, even standing so near the

blast of heat from the roaring fire. Now that the woman was safe, he needed to get out of his own damp clothes. Unbuttoning his shirt as he went, Jack returned to his bedroom.

He considered a hot shower, but didn't want to leave the woman that long. He made do with a brisk toweling dry, then pulled on jeans and a wool sweater. The propane heat had cycled on, taking the chill off the house as he returned to the great room with a fresh towel.

He knelt beside the unconscious woman and felt her pulse again. It had slowed to a steady rhythm, and her chest rose and fell evenly. A doctor ought to see her, but late on a Sunday evening, the hospital was the only option for medical care, and the nearest one was forty miles away. The roads were tricky even in the best weather; they'd be downright treacherous in this storm.

For the moment, keeping her dry and warm seemed the best course. If she didn't improve over the next hour or so, then he'd transport her up the hill to Tahoe Memorial.

His fingers probed along her skull, but his layman's examination didn't uncover any obvious bumps. He'd have to wait until she woke to ask if her head hurt. Using the towel, he did what he could to dry her hair, then tried to smooth it. If she was anything like Elizabeth, she'd be mortified by the bad-hair-day unruliness.

Except she was nothing like Elizabeth. His wife had been blond, her hair nearly to her waist, not a dark wedge like this woman's. Elizabeth's proportions were more generous, breasts full, hips and thighs softly rounded. She complained daily about the excess ten pounds she claimed she carried. But he had loved running his hand along those silky curves, seeing her smile with delight when he kissed her.

He shut down the memories, wouldn't let himself feel the pain that five years should have been enough to dull. Pulled himself back to the present and the woman lying beside his hearth.

She wasn't so much conventionally beautiful as she was striking. High cheekbones, full lips, narrow, determined chin. Her eyes seemed to slant ever so slightly upward. Were they green, an exotic contrast to her dark hair? Or dark chocolate like those still-damp strands clinging to her forehead?

And who was she? What brought her to his remote sanctuary? He supposed it was possible she'd made a wrong turn onto his road. But then, what happened to her car? If it skidded off the road, he would have seen signs of it on his way home. He supposed some of her injuries could have come from a car wreck.

Her face still felt cool to the back of his hand, although not as icy as when he first brought her inside. Was the rest of her warming up? He reached under the covers, brushing inadvertently against the bottom curve of one small breast. Heat rose in his cheeks. He felt a bit like a pervert copping a feel, but he had to know that her core temperature was rising.

His hand flattened across her rib cage, and relief filled him as he absorbed a faint warmth against his palm. She took a deeper breath, and he felt her chest rise against his hand. Her body shifted, pushing at the covers. He glanced at her face and had only an instant to register that her gray eyes were open and fixed on him.

Then she screamed.

She scrambled backward, fighting the constricting blankets as the man who had been touching her rose to his feet. Her back slammed against something, a chair. She huddled against it, then realized with horror that she was naked.

He turned his back to her. "Cover up. You have to stay warm."

She dragged the thick comforter over her, pressing herself against the chair. Her jeans and sweater were in a pile beside the recliner, her bra and panties by the fire. Despite the blazing fire, she started shivering, teeth chattering.

The man turned toward her again but kept his distance. Still, he seemed to loom over her, far too tall, his shoulders far too broad. His black hair brushed those wide shoulders. The hand he'd had resting against her stomach was frighteningly large.

She clutched the comforter tightly. "What did you do to me?"

"Rescued you." He shoved those powerful hands into the pockets of his jeans. "You fell into the creek."

She pushed the heel of her hand into her forehead and felt the dampness of her hair. As she ran her fingers through the unruly mess, the smell of creek water teased her nostrils. "Yes. I remember now." She shut down the instant replay her mind tried to offer. "Thank you."

"Sorry about your clothes, but I had to get you warm." He said it so matter-of-factly, as if he stripped unconscious women every day of the week.

Heat burned her cheeks. "Of course."

He took a step toward her, and she shrank back, fear coursing through her. But instead of drawing closer, he snagged a cushion from where she'd been lying by the fire and plopped it on the sofa.

He settled onto the cushion. "What the hell were you doing out here in the middle of nowhere?"

"I…" She scrubbed at her forehead again, shook her head. "That I don't remember. I was just…here. Pouring rain. Looking for help. I saw a light off in the distance."

"That would have to be this place, since there's no one else for miles around." He stretched his arm along the back of the sofa. She could still feel the imprint of his hand against her skin. "I'm Jack Traynor, by the way."

He stared at her expectantly, waiting for her to offer her own name. But the only thing playing through her mind was an endless loop of her fall into the creek. She squeezed her eyes shut, willed the spiraling images to stop.

"I'm..." She lifted her gaze to him, struggled to pull an answer from her still laboring brain. "I'm..."

"Who are you?" he asked, as if the explicit question might produce better results.

Tears pricked her eyes, tightened her throat. She could scarcely whisper her response. "I can't remember."

Chapter Two

"I can't remember who I am." She trembled, not from the cold anymore, but from rising panic. "I can't picture my own face. I don't even know what color my hair is."

She grabbed a handful, tried to pull it far enough forward to see. It was too short. She shook harder.

He was on his feet and at her side so quickly she didn't have time to be startled. He sank to the floor beside her, arms around her. She leaned back against his hard chest.

"Calm down. Take a slow breath. I don't want you going into shock."

Too overwhelmed by her loss of identity, she had no reserves left to be frightened by Jack. Instead his low voice rumbling in her ears soothed her, gave her strength. For the moment she let herself relax against him.

"I might have a name for you," he said. "Check your left ankle."

She poked her foot out from under the blanket. Raising her leg high enough to see, she made out "Mia" worked into the gold bracelet. "Is that my name?"

"Is it?" he asked.

She reached inside herself, groping through the emptiness for recognition. Her stomach lurched as her mind resisted. "It means nothing to me."

"I think we should assume it is."

Inwardly she rebelled against taking the alien name. But she had to call herself something. "I'm Mia, then."

He released her, shifting to face her, putting space between them. "Do you remember anything? Where you're from? Your parents' names? Brothers or sisters?"

She shook her head at each query. Her mind seemed wiped clean, as if she'd been born the moment she'd awakened beside the fire.

"Where were you born?" he asked. "What do you do for a living?"

The most elemental pieces of a person's life, yet she couldn't summon even one answer for Jack. "I don't know."

"What about your husband's name?"

"I'm not married." That response came quickly, without thinking.

Jack's gaze narrowed, then dropped to her left hand clutching the comforter. Nothing on her ring finger, but still, he asked, "How can you be so sure when you remember nothing else?"

"I'm not sure of anything." She breathed deeply, wincing at a tug of pain in her side. "That hurts."

"You were pretty banged up by debris in the creek."

He would know. He'd seen her naked. At this point he knew her body better than she did. "I want to get dressed." She sounded like a querulous child.

"You just regained consciousness. I don't want you getting up again."

"I can't just sit here with nothing on."

"You've got the comforter to keep you warm."

Yet even with the voluminous comforter, she felt exposed and far too vulnerable. "I just want to put my clothes back on."

"They're soaking wet."

She fought back tears. "Please," she whispered.

The slightest softness crept into his eyes. "Give me a minute. I'll put dry clothes in the bathroom for you."

He helped her to her feet and settled her in the recliner. She sagged in the chair once he'd left, dropping her head in her hands. She'd feel much better after she'd showered and dressed. But then what would she do? She could ask Jack Traynor to take her someplace, if only she knew where that place might be.

Hoping for distraction from her exhaustion, Mia looked around her. She'd never been inside a log home, seen how the interlocking timbers worked in the interior space. The vaulted beamed ceilings should have made the great room seem cavernous. But the grouping around the river-rock fireplace of sofa, recliner and side chair created a surprising coziness.

Jack emerged from a hallway off the entryway and started toward her. "Wait. Let me help you."

But she didn't want his hands on her again. Not because she was afraid of him. She just didn't like how weak she felt without her clothes.

She rose, clutching the thick covers tightly. She stumbled

slightly with her first few steps as she fought for balance, but shook off his hand when he offered it. "I'm fine."

Still, he walked alongside her. "Are you dizzy? If you are, you're lying down again, now."

"Not dizzy. Just a little tired."

He blocked the doorway of the bathroom before she could enter. "Did you hit your head when you fell? I couldn't feel a bump, but I'm no doctor."

The thought of those hands on her scalp, fingers gently prodding, sent a prickling along her spine. "I don't know." She ran her fingertips through her hair, wincing at three separate sore spots. "Must have."

"But you can't remember?"

Was that suspicion in his tone? "You think I'm making this up?"

He stared down at her, topping her by nearly a foot. He could be average height as far as she knew and she was just exceptionally short. But the way he seemed to dominate whatever space he occupied made her doubt that assessment.

She had to know. "How tall are you?"

Not a flicker of reaction in his face at the odd question. "Six-four."

"How tall am I?"

He angled in close. Too close. Moved a measuring hand from the top of her head to an inch below his chin. "Maybe five-six."

"How old…" Her throat went dry. "How old do you think I am?" Why did it matter? She just felt compelled to fill in those crucial blanks.

"Late twenties?"

She nodded, taking that in. "What's the date?"

She wondered at the grief in his eyes. "December fourteenth."

Her relief surprised her. "I think I knew that." She smiled. "Only another week or so, then."

She heard a trace of anger in his tone. "Until what?"

"Christmas. What else?"

He shook his head, moving out of the bathroom doorway. "Go take your shower. Yell if you get into trouble."

She moved inside, locking the door and leaning against it. Releasing the comforter and afghan to pool around her ankles, she stepped free and turned to face the wide mirror over the double sink.

God, she was skinny. Small breasts, hip bones sticking out, collarbone prominent. From her build, she seemed naturally thin, but her body seemed so spare, she wondered if she'd been sick. The red marks on her stomach and her legs just added to the generally unhealthy look of her. The two-inch-long scratch on her left arm was a lurid crimson against the too-pale skin.

Staring at her body allowed her to delay focusing on her face. She wanted desperately to recognize herself, was terrified she wouldn't. Nothing in the lines of her slender body brought enlightenment. She had no choice but to lift her gaze higher.

A stranger looked back at her. Eyes a somber gray, hair dark brown, pasted to her skull where it wasn't sticking out at crazy right angles. Cheeks nearly gaunt, adding to that underfed look. Was she anorexic?

Tired of racking her brain for answers that it refused to produce, she turned from the mirror. Bending over carefully, wary of making herself dizzy, she unclasped the ankle bracelet. She started to put it on top of the vanity, but it crossed her mind she might knock it into the sink and down the drain. Opening a drawer, she dropped it inside.

A second door in the bathroom led to the shower and commode. She closed that door, as well, glad to have an additional barrier of safety. That brought her up short for a moment, started her wondering why she thought she needed the extra protection.

Jack had left a stack of clothes on the back of the commode—T-shirt, bright blue sweatshirt, matching sweatpants, white socks. Beside them he'd placed a three-pack of woman's panties with a price sticker still on it. A wife's or girlfriend's? She'd seen no sign of anyone here but him. She smiled when she saw the neatly folded bra under the panties. A D cup. There was her proof he hadn't taken a very good look at her. Her tiny breasts would never fill those roomy cups.

Cranking the spigot as hot as it would go, she sat on the edge of the tub and considered a bath instead of a shower. Lying down would be easier than standing under the spray. But she felt nauseous at the thought of being submerged in water.

Images suddenly overwhelmed her. Her body pounded, twisted and spun. A blow to her midsection, several to her legs. Deadfall in the water, he'd said. Yet even here, when she was perfectly safe, the fragmented memories filled her with fear.

She couldn't remember anything else of herself, her life, even how tall she was, for God's sake. Yet those brief moments in the water dominated her brain, as if nothing else had happened to her before or since.

With an effort she shook off the dark images as she positioned herself under the shower spray. And prayed she'd somehow get her life back.

Jack brought in the last load of groceries from the truck and carried the two bags into the kitchen. Setting them beside the others on the black granite countertop, he listened for the sound of the shower. It had taken her a few minutes to turn the water on, so it had only been running for maybe five. Even using hot water, he doubted she'd want to be wet for very long.

Unexpected images intruded in his mind—Mia's body arched under the shower spray, hands running along her skin as she washed herself. Him pulling back the shower curtain, stepping inside to press a kiss against her throat, to run gentle fingers along the curve of her small breasts.

He slammed a lid on his wayward thoughts as the shower shut off. What the hell was he thinking? When he'd undressed Mia, it had been awkward and embarrassing despite the necessity of his actions. With her unconscious—obviously in distress—his body had had no reaction to her nakedness. But with her awake, still unquestionably in distress but with some fight surfacing in her, he'd responded to her as he would any woman.

Just a normal reaction, he told himself as he efficiently stowed groceries and supplies in the kitchen, garage freezer and pantry. Except for the fact that his libido had been in hiding for months now. Maybe a consequence of living in isolation too long, only venturing into the "real world" as needed for his engineering consulting business. Maybe because it was just simpler to avoid the entanglements of personal relationships. After Elizabeth's death and the disaster of Joanna Sanchez, he had refused to let himself be vulnerable that way again.

Whatever the reason, his attraction for Mia was entirely inappropriate. She needed someone to keep her safe for the night, not lust after her body. Hopefully, the weather would clear up enough so he could drive her into town tomorrow. They'd locate her car on the way out and arrange for a tow-truck driver. Likely as not her ID would be in the vehicle, as well. That might be enough to jog her memory.

The two weeks' worth of groceries put away, he laid out a box of linguini, jar of sauce and a pair of frozen chicken breasts. As he filled a pot with water for the pasta, he listened for sounds from the bathroom. The silence made him uneasy. Setting the pot on the stove and twisting on the gas, he crossed the great room to the hall. Ear pressed to the bathroom door, he strained to hear her moving inside.

Nothing. "Mia?" he called out. No answer. "Mia!" he shouted.

Still no response. Could she have stumbled getting out of the shower and hit her head? Or simply collapsed with exhaustion? Either way, she'd need his help.

He pounded on the door, yelling out, "Mia, I'm coming in!" When she didn't protest, he tried the knob, then grabbed the key he kept above the door on the edge of the molding.

He let himself in, his first glance taking in his comforter in a mound on the floor and the closed door to the shower area. Maybe she hadn't heard him yelling, knocking? Was she using the toilet?

He shouted her name again, then knocked. His heart pounding in the silence, he turned the knob. The door caught on something—her legs. Through the six-inch crack, he could see her, dressed in Elizabeth's sweatsuit, sitting on the closed toilet seat and leaning against the wall.

When he nudged her with the door, she shifted her legs, making way for him even in her sleep. Relief surged through him that she hadn't lost consciousness again. But she still slumped against the dividing wall, eyes closed, breathing deeply.

He shook her shoulder, but she didn't waken. She tried to

turn away from him, her face scrunching like a petulant child's. Obviously, she'd expended whatever energy her adrenaline had given her just showering and getting dressed. Although she probably needed to eat, for the moment it would be best to let her sleep.

As he lifted her carefully, he noticed the bra on the back of the toilet. He'd known Elizabeth hadn't been anywhere near Mia's size. Why had he given it to her? Because Mia without a bra gave him far too much to think about. Especially now with her pressed against his chest, warm and relaxed in his arms. His soap and shampoo smelled different on her, more floral, enigmatic.

Ignoring the intriguing fragrance, he carried Mia to the guest room and laid her on one side of the queen-size bed. Hurrying around the bed, he pulled back the covers, then transferred her carefully. As he arranged the sheet and comforter over her, she barely stirred, just snuggled deeper into the pillow.

Returning to the kitchen to turn off the stove, he paced the room trying to figure out what to do next. Ordinarily on a Sunday evening, he'd catch up on reading his technical magazines, watch a little television, maybe tinker with one of the electronic toys he created as a hobby. Knowing he had errands to run today, he'd had a long visit via Web cam with William Franklin yesterday. For the past six months Jack had been mentoring William, a boy as scary brilliant at age eight as Jack himself had been.

Of course, this wasn't an ordinary Sunday evening. Not with the anniversary looming, with all the pain and grief that went with it. Ten days away, he still had fair control of his emotions, but the memories had started chewing at his insides. Maybe the distraction Mia provided wasn't so bad.

Grabbing a stack of magazines from the great room, he moved back toward the guest bedroom. It wouldn't hurt to keep an eye on her until she woke again. She might need something, and he might not hear her call out if he was in the great room or his office. He could read in the guest room as well as he could anywhere else.

Sliding the two months' worth of a half-dozen magazines onto the nightstand, he scooted an armchair from the corner toward the bed. She'd turned in her sleep so that she faced him, her lips parted slightly, her cheeks showing more color than when he'd first placed her beside the hearth.

He remembered watching Elizabeth sleep. In those early days, after he'd taught his last class at U.C. Berkeley, he'd work so late at the lab he leased in Oakland she would be in bed when he got home. He was on strict orders to wake her and usually he did, as eager as she for time together. But sometimes he sat on the edge of the bed in their cramped Berkeley apartment and listened to her breathe, watching her chest rise and fall, guessing at her dreams.

He'd thought they'd have decades together, not seven short years. If he'd known, he would have held her tighter, told her more often he loved her.

Mia let out a long sigh, drawing his attention to the pixie-haired stranger. If he were one to always look for symbolism and significance as Elizabeth had been, he might have interpreted Mia's sudden appearance in his life as auspicious, rather than mere coincidence. Maybe even a message from Elizabeth herself, dug from his subconscious.

But five years after her death, there was only one message he would welcome. *It was all a mistake, love. I'm still alive.*

* * *

Mia woke to the smell of something tantalizing cooking in the kitchen. Pushing aside the heavy covers, she puzzled over how she'd ended up in bed. She remembered dressing after her shower, sinking onto the lid of the commode to rest for just a moment. Leaning against the wall and closing her eyes.

He had to have carried her in here. As she eased herself to the edge of the bed, every muscle screaming, she spotted the chair pulled up close. A magazine on the chair, pages folded back marking his place, told her he'd been sitting here with her for some time.

She squinted at the digital clock on the nightstand. Nearly 8:00 p.m. She'd slept for three hours. If she'd dreamed, if her mind had given her clues to her identity during REM, she could recall nothing now.

Her body ached abominably as she rose, but her stomach and her nose pulled her from the room. She'd never felt so ravenous. No telling when she'd eaten last. Based on the leanness of her body, whatever she had eaten hadn't been enough.

He stood at the stove, his back to her as she traced the delectable aroma to the kitchen. She hesitated in the doorway, watching him lift the sauté pan from the stove and, with an expert flex of his wrist, flip the slices of chicken in it. A large pot of water simmered on a back burner, and a thick red sauce bubbled in another pan up front.

He flicked a glance in her direction. "How are you feeling?"

"Like a truck fell on me." She inched into the kitchen, the tile floor cool even through the thick socks she wore. "That smells divine."

"My take on chicken piccata." He pointed to a cabinet near

the sink. "There's ibuprofen on the second shelf. Glasses in the cabinet next to the fridge."

She shook out two of the painkillers, then got some water from the tap. As she swallowed the pills, Jack fanned a box of linguini into the boiling water. He stirred the pasta as it relaxed into the pot, then set aside the spoon and faced her.

"You'll have to spend the night," he said. "If the weather cooperates, I'll drive you up to the sheriff's substation in South Lake Tahoe. County sheriff can take it from there."

Her stomach knotted, and sudden panic prickled through her. She struggled to ignore it. "I appreciate you letting me stay."

He stabbed at the pasta again with the black plastic spoon. "On our way out, we'll look for your car."

"What car?"

"You had to get here somehow. The creek is four miles from the highway. Did you walk all that way up my road?"

She rubbed her brow. "I remember walking. But not on the road, not at first. Just through the forest. It took me a while to find the road."

He narrowed his gaze on her. "However you got into those woods, you had to have started out in a car. We'll find it tomorrow."

She tried to picture herself behind the wheel, winding her way up that steep gravel road. But she couldn't even visualize what kind of car she drove, let alone remember herself behind the wheel.

Edgy and anxious, she asked, "Can I do anything?"

"There's some bagged lettuce in the fridge, bottled dressing in the door. Feel free to add whatever you like to the salad."

She quickly found the lettuce, then fished tomatoes and a ripe avocado from the crisper door. She added a jar of kalamata olives and carton of feta cheese to the items on the granite countertop.

Without waiting for instruction, she opened cupboards until she found a salad bowl, then slid out a cutting board from beside the knife block. She selected a serrated knife, stood with it poised over the bright red tomato.

Her hand shook. Her throat closed. Her chest felt so tight she couldn't breathe. Her fingers squeezed the taut skin of the tomato until her nails broke through, expelling juice onto the wooden cutting board. Fear stabbed through her at the sight of those thin red dribbles pooling beside her hand. An image flashed in her mind—her hand gripping the scratch on her left arm, blood oozing from between her fingers.

"Mia."

The voice echoed through her skull as if her head had emptied of content. Her mind had floated off, seeping from her head, hovering over her. Somehow she was outside herself, watching herself stand there, holding the knife, crushing the tomato in her fingers.

"Mia!"

This time she registered the voice as Jack's, became aware of his hand wrapped around her wrist. Terror rocketed through her in reaction to his powerful grip, and she tried to pull away. But he didn't relent, shouting her name as he held on, the name that meant nothing to her.

"Let go of the knife, Mia!"

At his shouted command, she looked dully down at their joined hands. Saw the way her index finger had shifted too far up the handle and now curled around the blade. Deep red droplets joined the puddling tomato juice on the cutting board.

With a gasp, she flung the knife away. Jack gentled his hold on her, then guided her to the sink. He cranked on the cold water and held her hand under its flow.

"Don't move," he barked, leaving her side long enough to turn off the burners.

She stared down at the thinning blood as the water diluted it. Still with that sense of distant observation, she realized it wasn't much of a cut. She'd only caught the edge of the knife, and despite her frozen grip, hadn't pressed it in too deeply.

She turned off the water and grabbed a paper towel. Only a dab of blood welled from the cut. A little pressure would stanch the flow.

Jack bracketed her face with his large hands. "You're as white as a sheet."

His touch grounded her, driving the fog from her brain. She shook her head, enjoying the feel of him moving with her. "I'm fine."

"The hell you are." He dropped his hands. "I'm going to assume you just need to eat. You're nothing but skin and bones."

The assessment stung, despite the simple truth of it. Heat rising in her cheeks, she took a step toward the counter where she'd left the makings of the salad.

Jack intervened. "I'll do that. You sit down. There's bread on the table. I want you to eat some with plenty of butter."

She was too desperate for something to eat to waste the energy for argument. She pulled back one of the chairs where he'd laid a place setting and helped herself to a thick slice of French bread from the basket. As she slathered it generously with butter, Jack drained the pasta, then turned to assemble the salad.

He threw away the ruined tomato and opened the refrigerator for a replacement. He took it in his hand and placed it on the counter.

"No," Mia said, more loudly than she'd intended. "No tomato, please."

Jack gave her a long look. "You don't like them?"

"Yes. No. Dammit, I don't know. Just don't put it in the salad."

With a nod, he put it back in the crisper drawer. As she choked down a bite of bread, Mia swiped away the fragments of memory that still swirled in her mind—anger, blood, pain. She knew she should be trying to remember, should force those images into awareness. But for the moment, she'd just as soon not know what darkness lurked in her past.

Chapter Three

After two helpings of chicken, a full plate of pasta, a healthy serving of salad and more bread, Mia's head felt clearer. It seemed as if she hadn't eaten properly for a good long while and needed to make up for lost time. Still, as she ate she felt twinges of anxiety—was she eating too much? Would she get too fat? She pushed aside the nagging messages as she ate, driven on by her body's imperative.

Jack let her help carry the dishes in from the dining-room table, but when she tried to rinse her plate, he plucked it from her hands and pointed her toward a bar stool pulled up to the breakfast bar. He made quick work of slotting plates and flatware into the dishwasher, then washing the cookware he'd used.

"Stay there," he ordered as he shut off the water and strode from the kitchen.

The moment he was out of sight, she slid from the stool.

He'd left the bread basket on the table with a couple slices of French bread still in it. No sense in letting it go stale; she'd find a plastic bag and put it away.

She found the bags in the third drawer she opened. Slipping one out, she turned too swiftly back toward the dining room. Her head swam, sparkles of light dancing in her vision as she groped for the nearest counter. But the bag was still in that hand and the slick plastic gave her no purchase on the polished granite.

She stumbled, banging her shin against the kitchen trash can, no doubt adding to the collection of bruises there. Before she could regain her balance, she felt his hands on her, righting her. With firm determination he plunked her down into a dining-room chair. He set a white-and-blue first-aid box beside her.

"I told you to sit still," he said, a trace of irritation in his tone.

"I wanted to put the bread away." She gestured at the basket.

He grabbed the plastic bag from the counter and tucked the slices in it. "Push up your left sleeve." He opened the box and laid out hydrogen peroxide, a tube of ointment, gauze and tape, then pulled a chair over for himself.

She shoved the sleeve up past her elbow. "Whose clothes are these?"

He dabbed hydrogen peroxide on her arm, and it foamed along the scratch. "My wife's."

"Is she—"

"She's dead." He squeezed a line of antibiotic ointment on a square of gauze and pressed it to her arm.

"I'm sorry."

"A long time ago."

His long, capable fingers held the gauze steady as he affixed it with tape. His gentleness melted something inside her, a knot of fear she hadn't even known she still harbored. With his head bent so close to her, she could look up at him side-long and study him surreptitiously.

He'd tucked his long, black hair behind his ears, revealing high cheekbones that could have been Native American. His eyes were nearly as dark as his hair and were opaque as if they concealed secrets. The sensuality of his full mouth, despite the grim line he now held it in, stirred her imagination. What would it be like to have that mouth pressed against the crook of her arm, along her throat? Or trailing a line of moist kisses across her collarbone, down between her breasts…

As if he'd read her mind, he lifted his gaze to hers. Those dark eyes, so fathomless, seemed to bore into her soul, searching for the truth buried there. If he really could ferret out her identity, she should be grateful. But she felt as stripped bare emotion-ally by his probing gaze as she'd been naked to him physically.

He released her arm and abruptly rose. "Go to bed. You need a good night's rest."

While he replaced the contents of the first-aid box, Mia eased herself up. The spurt of energy she'd felt after dinner had faded and she wanted nothing more than to crawl back into that bed. But she wasn't used to being ordered around.

She wasn't? How could she know that, when she remem-bered nothing else? She had a sense of being in control, being in charge. Being the one to give the orders.

She thought about her reflection in the mirror—skinny, almost frail. It didn't jibe with her more-powerful mental image of herself.

Still, it rankled to simply march off to bed, obedient as a child. When he finished with the first-aid box and fixed her with his stare, she just stared back.

"How long were you married?" she asked.

Silence beat for several seconds. He turned away before he answered, setting the box on the black granite countertop. "Seven years."

"How long ago did she…"

He turned toward her again, that beautiful mouth compressed tightly. "Let's stick to figuring out who you are, not who I am."

He walked out of the kitchen. Mia followed, watched him cross the great room into what she guessed was the master bedroom. She made her way to the guest room, tiredness weighing heavily with each step. Shifting aside the magazine, she sank into the chair beside the bed.

Her eyes shut, she didn't know he'd entered the room until he spoke. "I thought you'd need these."

His hands were wrapped around a satiny pink bundle. He set the pile on the bed.

"A pair of Elizabeth's pajamas. She only wore them once or twice. Too big for you, I'm guessing, but it's the best I can do." He fished something out from the pajamas. "A new toothbrush and toothpaste. Will you need anything else?"

Answers, she thought. "No, thank you."

Edging around her, he gathered up his magazines. "You're okay getting dressed on your own?" Color rose in his cheeks as he asked the question.

She felt a flush rise in her own cheeks. "Yes. I'm fine."

He retraced his steps from the room but then hesitated by the door. "It's been five years," he said. Then he walked out, leaving her alone.

Magazines piled on the sofa beside him, Jack stared moodily at the dying embers in the pellet stove, all too aware of the woman sleeping just a couple dozen feet away. After she'd finished in the bathroom, he'd wandered over toward the guest room a few times, looking for the light under her door. She'd switched it off an hour ago, and when he'd checked ten minutes later, she was asleep.

He didn't let himself stay there, watching her as he'd done earlier. He felt dangerously vulnerable already, so near the anniversary. The last thing he needed was to start fantasizing about Mia's body and how it might feel under his hands, his mouth.

Ministering to the scratch on her arm, despite the necessity of it, had been a mistake. What should have been a clinical cleansing and bandaging had been transformed by his over-fertile imagination into a sensual experience. He'd let himself enjoy the silky texture of her skin against his fingers, the warmth of her, the faint scent of her freshly washed hair.

He closed the magazine on his lap and tossed it aside. It wasn't quite eleven and he rarely went to sleep before midnight. But he couldn't stand to sit still any longer, pretending to read. He pushed to his feet and headed for his office, switching off lights as he went.

His satellite Internet link was sometimes iffy in a storm of the magnitude of the one still roaring outside. If he couldn't connect to the Web, he'd have to resort to one of the DVDs stacked beside the entertainment unit in the master suite. He doubted a movie, no matter how riveting, would keep him focused tonight.

But he had no trouble connecting to a search site. As the wind moaned outside, rain spattering against the windows, he typed in "Mia" and "missing." It was just an initial foray; he'd have to add other search terms to narrow down the results.

As he scanned page one of the million-plus hits, he realized for the first time the irony of Mia's name. MIA. Missing in Action. If there was any information on the World Wide Web about a missing woman named Mia, it was drowned in the hundreds of thousands of Internet pages about missing soldiers.

So engrossed was he in flipping through the pages of search hits, he didn't hear her enter his office, her bare feet silent on the thick carpet. When her hand gripped the back of his chair, he swung around to look up at her. She stared at the screen, her gray eyes wide with fear. Had she just woken from a nightmare?

"What are you doing?" she asked, knuckles white where she gripped the chair.

"Seeing what I can find out about you."

She'd gone so pale, he worried about her passing out again. The pink satin pajamas, far too large for her, seemed to shrink her into a fragile doll.

Rising, he peeled her hand from the back of the chair. "Sit down."

She resisted him, keeping her gaze riveted on the screen. "You can't…please don't…" She pushed past him, reaching for the mouse. She clicked the *X* in the upper-right corner, and the Internet browser vanished.

She all but collapsed into the chair. Jack went down on one knee and took her hands. They were icy. Her breathing was more rapid than he liked and he could see the tension that fear had put into her face.

"What is it, Mia? What am I not supposed to do?"

She shook her head, as if to pull herself from a daze. "Don't look for me."

"I thought you wanted to find out who you are."

"I do." Her brow furrowed. "It makes sense to search the

Internet." She shook her head again slowly. "But the thought of what you'll find terrifies me."

Her hands, so small in his, had warmed, her fingers curled within his own. She turned her wrists, her thumbs curving around his as if to anchor herself. He closed his hands around hers more snugly.

Her shoulders slumping, she tipped her head down, the fragrance of his own shampoo in her hair alchemized into something mysterious and intriguing. He could feel her trembling, and he tugged her closer, wrapping his arms around her.

A big mistake. The slick feel of the satiny pajamas brought back vague memories of Elizabeth, of holding her just as he held Mia. The memories intertwined, except it wasn't Elizabeth's thick blond hair he longed to bury his face in, it was Mia's short silky cap. Mia's ear he wanted to brush his mouth along, Mia's sensitive lobe he wanted to taste.

He pulled away from her. "You should get back to bed."

She looked up at him. "You won't do any more searches?"

What did it matter? She'd be gone in the morning, anyway. He might as well leave it to the county sheriff. "I won't."

She flattened a hand on his desk to push herself to her feet. He grabbed for her when she swayed, then held her elbow as he walked her back to the guest room. Her exhaustion squelched his errant thoughts. He got her back into bed without doing anything stupid.

Returning to his office, he switched off the lights. A novel waited for him on his nightstand, one of the latest hot thrillers. Maybe he could read himself to sleep.

When he saw the stripped bed, he remembered the comforter he'd wrapped Mia in after he'd undressed her. She'd left it and the afghan in a heap in the bathroom, likely too enervated to fold them. He threw the afghan into the laundry room, then carried the comforter back to his room.

The side that had been wrapped around her was only slightly damp, the afghan having wicked up most of the moisture from her body. It made sense to spread it across his bed and let it completely air dry. The fact that Mia's fragrance still lingered in the fabric had nothing to do with it.

He knew his justifications were nothing but BS. Even still, after he showered and pulled on pajama bottoms—more than he usually wore, but she might need him during the night—he climbed under the comforter. He had to push it aside to keep from overheating even in the coolness of his bedroom. But the edge of it was only inches from his face, and he couldn't help but inhale Mia's subtle scent.

He barely read a page before his eyes grew heavy. Switching off the light, he dropped immediately into sleep, dreams of Elizabeth fading into images of Mia.

Pale sunlight slanting into Mia's face woke her. Still drowsy, she blinked at the dancing dust motes and struggled to work out where she was. Jack's house, she remembered. Safe in his guest room. Warmth filled her at the thought.

She relaxed against the pillow, eyes closed. She drifted back into a half sleep, and for the briefest moment the answers to who and what and why seemed to dance just out of reach. If she lay still, held her breath, reached carefully toward them, she would know everything.

But before she could touch those evanescent memories, something intruded between her and her past, something dark and frightening looming in her mind's eye. She moaned in her semidream state, her heart hammering in her chest.

Her body lay frozen; she was unable to pull herself free of that menace.

With a jolt she came fully awake, her field of view filled with Jack leaning over her, his large, gentle hands on her shoulders. Now she registered him calling her name, realized it was Jack who had pulled her to consciousness and safety.

The points of contact where he touched her sent warmth seeping into her shoulders, meandering down her spine. She wanted to run her hands along his arms, stroke the hair-roughened skin from wrists to elbows where he'd pushed up the sleeves of his black turtleneck. Her breathing had slowed after the scare of her nightmare, but now it quickened as she imagined how those ropy muscles would feel under her palms.

His dark gaze dropped to her mouth. His head bent toward her fractionally, as if in preparation to lower it to hers, to kiss her. Her lips parted in anticipation.

He snatched his hands away as if she'd burned him. "Your clothes are on the dresser. Breakfast in five minutes." He backed away from the bed, then strode from the room.

She lay there, stunned, wondering what in heaven's name she could have been thinking. He wasn't about to kiss her. Her head must have still been foggy from sleep to have imagined something so crazy.

Throwing back the covers, she rose from the bed. Jack had left the bedroom door partly open, and when she inhaled, her mouth watered at the aroma of coffee, bacon and toast. Her stomach kicked into overdrive, persuading her to get moving.

On the dresser, Mia found her freshly laundered jeans and another T-shirt and sweatshirt. A well-worn pair of sneakers two sizes too large were on the floor. Her bra and panties were on the dresser, as well, but the bra was torn so badly, it was unusable. She was small enough to do without.

The image of Jack washing her intimates, the silky scraps dwarfed by his large hands, sent a shiver rippling down her spine. She quashed the unwanted sensation as she gathered up the pile of clothes, tossing the bra into the trash.

Where was her wool sweater? she wondered as she crossed to the bathroom. Maybe it hadn't survived the dunking in the creek. Regret flickered through her at the thought that Jack might have thrown it away without asking her. She had only the vaguest memory of what the sweater looked like, but it meant something to her nevertheless.

As she stripped out of the pajamas and donated panties, she saw the bruises in the bathroom mirror. The angry red marks on her legs, her stomach, had faded overnight into a pale purple blue. As she twisted behind her in the bathroom mirror she caught a glimpse of the splotches on her back from her trapezius to just above her glutes. One on her lower back had purpled even darker. Had her back struck the railing that hard as she fell?

She dithered for a moment after she'd dressed, reluctant to face Jack again. Could he have seen the expectation in her eyes? Was that why he'd withdrawn so abruptly? The possibility filled her with mortification.

Her stomach didn't care how embarrassed she felt, grumbling its demand to be filled. She'd just have to pretend that moment in the bed had never happened.

Folding the pajamas, she set them on the foot of the bed then headed toward the kitchen. The too-large sneakers flopped on her feet as she went.

She found Jack stirring eggs at the stove. A plate piled high with bacon sat on the dining-room table beside a carton of orange-mango juice. A check of the bread basket revealed triangles of buttered toast.

"Scrambled eggs okay?" Jack asked as he shut off the stove.

"I'm starving." She took a toast triangle and slice of bacon and rolled the strip up into the bread. Seating herself at the table, she munched as she waited for Jack to bring the eggs over.

Two plates in his hands, he gave her an odd look. "Do you always do that?"

Her mouth full, she looked down at the rolled bread. "I have no idea. I didn't even think before I did it."

Setting down the plates, he sat beside her. "Any change since yesterday?"

She served herself more bacon and toast, then scooped up a forkful of eggs. "This morning, when I was half dozing, I thought I might remember. But I think it was just a dream, a trick of my mind."

"Have you thought about what you're going to do when I take you to the sheriff?"

Fear prickled inside her. "How can they even help if I don't know who I am?"

"They'll check their missing-persons database, look for a match. If there's nothing local, they'll notify other agencies. I'm sure someone who knows you will come forward."

She should be relieved at the prospect. Instead, terror mounted inside her. She swallowed a mouthful of toast and bacon with difficulty. The darkness she'd found so frightening in her dream seemed to hover on the periphery, waiting for its chance.

Jack poured her some juice, although she didn't see how she would force any down her throat. Her stomach, just a moment ago clamoring for food, roiled.

"Maybe we'll find your car on the way down the hill," Jack said. His gaze fixed all too perceptively on her. "We'd be able to ID you positively."

She sat stock-still, staring down at her plate, hands gripping the table. Tears felt perilously close, although she didn't understand why. Hand trembling, she picked up her juice and with an effort pushed some past her tight throat.

With Jack's gaze on her, Mia left most of the eggs on her plate, as well as the toast and bacon she'd served herself. He didn't comment as he picked up her nearly full plate and set it by the sink. Too distressed to offer help, she watched him wordlessly as he tidied up.

He was ready to leave far too quickly, gathering up his keys and ushering her to the garage. Once he'd settled her in his truck and opened the garage door, he started the engine, ready to pull out.

He shoved the car back into Park. "Forgot something."

She huddled in her seat as he hurried back inside. When he returned, he held a red bundle against his chest.

He handed her the bundle. "I was afraid to put it in the dryer, so it's still a little damp."

She unfolded the red sweater, saw the cheery snowman and Christmas tree knitted into the front and burst into tears.

Chapter Four

Jack didn't think. He just leaned across the center console and pulled Mia into his arms. She sagged against him, her body trembling as she sobbed. The soft sound of her tears set off an ache in his chest, made him want to roar at the universe for hurting her.

Elizabeth, sweet, sensible and down-to-earth, rarely cried. The few times she did—when her mother died, when she learned from her doctor that she was barren—it broke his heart. He'd held her in his arms just as he did Mia.

"What is it?" he asked her when she quieted.

He felt her shake her head against his shoulder. "I don't know. The sweater. I was just so glad to see it."

"Did it spark a memory?" he asked.

Her fingers worked against the knit of his wool sweater,

and he fought to suppress a shudder. "No," she said finally. "It means nothing to me. It just seems…important."

She took a long breath, her chest swelling briefly against his, then pulled away from him. He found himself reluctant to let her go. Regretted the necessity of her leaving, of her stepping out of his life as precipitously as she'd entered it.

She was a stranger; why should she matter to him? Jack pressed the button on the garage remote and started the truck. He backed the Suburban into the sullen, damp December morning.

"I can take you up into Tahoe or down into Placerville," he told her as he turned the truck and headed down the driveway. "County sheriff has an office in both locations."

"Whatever's closer," she said, slumping back in her seat. She clutched the sweater in her hands.

He'd take her up Highway 50 to South Lake Tahoe, then to the office there. They'd file any necessary reports, contact other agencies, help her with any medical care she needed. She'd be in good hands.

He imagined walking away from her at the sheriff's office, driving the truck back home with the seat beside him empty. Despair bloomed inside him, a loneliness he thought he'd conquered years ago.

It's the anniversary, he told himself. *It's got you off balance.*

They reached the bridge, littered with deadfall and gravel washed up by the rain-swollen creek. Jack stopped the truck to clear away some of the larger tree limbs, tossing them on the downhill side of the bank. When he climbed back into the truck, Mia sat rigid in her seat, her fingers gripping the sweater so tightly, the skin over her knuckles was blanched white.

"You're okay," he told her as he put the truck in gear. "You're safe."

As he bumped across to the other side, skidding a little in the rain-sodden mud, she shut her eyes briefly, her chest rising and falling as she breathed. They left the bridge behind, and her hands relaxed in her lap.

He wanted to reach over, link his fingers with hers, maintain that contact for the short time they had together. It made no sense. It would be foolhardy in any case, dangerous. In the stretch ahead, the road down grew steeper, the mountainside dropping away precipitously on the right and towering in a sheer face on the left. That section of road always required careful driving.

But he couldn't resist another glance over at her, an impulse that nearly was their undoing. He glimpsed the sudden fear on her face an instant before he faced forward and slammed on the brakes. The truck fishtailed to a stop inches from a wall of rock and mud.

"Dammit." Jack stared at the landslide across his road, assessing quickly that there was no getting past it.

Her cheeks were far too pale, her eyes too wide as they stared out the windshield. "Is there an alternate route to the highway?"

He laughed mirthlessly. "No."

She glanced at him, the alarm plain in her face. "How do we get out?"

"We don't. As unstable as that mess is, it's too risky to try to cross it. Until it's cleared away—" he clenched his teeth so tight, his jaw ached "—we're trapped here."

She shoved open her door, and before he could stop her, she slid from the truck, leaving the red sweater behind on the seat. Jack shut off the engine and hurried after her. He caught up to her beside the tumbled edge of rock, mud and gravel that filled the roadbed. When she would have climbed onto the face of the slide, he grabbed her arm, pulling her back.

"You can't walk on that. It's not stable."

"There has to be a way to go around it." She tugged against him. He hated tightening his grip on her, but he didn't dare let her go.

"No way around it, Mia. Not even a four-wheel-drive truck could drive along that hillside. It would just get stuck in the muck if I tried to go over, and we'd risk bringing more of it down on us."

Her teeth chattered in the chill. "I want to go home." Her sharp intake of breath was more sob than inhalation. "But I don't even know where that is."

He loosened his fingers, ready to clamp down again if she tried to bolt. But the panic seemed to have eased.

She wrapped her arms around herself. "What do we do now?"

"We go back to the house and I call my friend Dawson, arrange for a crew to come out and clear the road."

She nodded, but still, she didn't move. His hand on her shoulder, he turned her away from the rockslide.

"We should get back to the truck. We're vulnerable as long as we're here." The hillside, wet with mud, loomed above them. "We damn well don't want the truck buried if it lets loose again."

Not to mention how cold it was, between the drizzle and the sinking temperatures. The brief sunshine of early morning had given way again to overcast. The last thing he needed was to have Mia get sick on top of everything else.

As they retraced their steps, Mia stared at the downhill side of the road. "It took some trees with it."

The rockslide had stripped saplings and shrubs from a swath of the mountainside both above and below. The broken trees and manzanita studded the field of mud and rocks.

"A mudslide can accelerate to upwards of thirty-five miles an hour." She shuddered as cold air gusted past them. "Considering how steep that hillside is, this one probably moved that fast."

Her ears were reddening in the cold, making him want to nestle her against him to warm her. The near constant compulsion to touch her set him on edge.

He wrenched the door to the truck open for her. "How do you know that?" he demanded. "You can't remember anything else, but you know so damn much about landslides."

"I don't know." The confusion in her face was clear as he helped her into her seat. "It just popped into my mind."

He went around the back of the Suburban, grabbing a blanket stowed behind the third seat. He threw it over Mia, then backed the truck out of the danger zone. Retreating around the curve, he looked for a spot wide enough to turn around in.

He cranked up the heater, and Mia held her hands out to the warmth blowing from the vents. The blanket tucked up under her chin, she sat silently, her wounded gaze on the sodden trees alongside the road. She made only one noise as they jounced along, a gasp of fear when they fishtailed badly right before the bridge. It took everything in him to keep driving, to resist the impulse to pull her into his arms, soothe her fear.

She finally spoke as they pulled up the last stretch of road to the house. "How long will it take?"

He pulled back into the garage and waited until the automatic door had shut before he answered. "I won't know until I talk to Dawson."

"Is Dawson in construction?"

"He's my chief operating officer." At her blank look, he elaborated, "I run an engineering firm from my house. Mostly municipal projects, water storage and delivery, that sort of thing. Dawson's the face of Traynor Engineering."

He wasn't sure if she'd even absorbed his explanation. She still had that lost look on her face and was shivering as they stepped inside the house. Either cold or emotions shook her slender body; in any case, he wanted her sitting in front of the fire ASAP.

His hand splayed across the middle of her back, and he nudged her toward the pellet stove. Despite the layers of fabric between his skin and hers, he could so easily imagine her heat.

"I'm fine," she said through chattering teeth as he urged her along.

"Right."

She hugged herself, determination surfacing in her face, belying her seeming fragility. Jack thought she would have held back her body's trembling with sheer will if it was possible.

He opened a small door beside the pellet stove to reveal a control panel. She might as well know how to operate it if she was going to be here a few days.

"You press this button to start it." He stabbed the round green button. "You make the fire hotter by adjusting the fuel feed. This is the fan speed." He arrowed up those buttons as high as they would go.

Dragging the recliner closer to the pellet stove, he pointed to the chair. "Sit."

About to retrieve the afghan throw from the dryer, he remembered the blankets stored in Elizabeth's hope chest. Set under the window seat that overlooked the yard, the hope chest was handier than the laundry room. The blankets inside might be musty, but they were warm, thick wool.

Grabbing a brightly colored Navaho blanket from the chest, he dropped it in Mia's lap. It wouldn't be wise to tuck it around her himself. His memory of wrapping the afghan around Mia's wet body last night were still all too clear.

"I'll be right back."

Nodding, she kept her gaze fixed on the flames already flickering through the glass window of the pellet stove. Her teeth had stopped chattering, but the cold and emotional upheaval had taken their toll after the ravaging her body had experienced the day before. Exhaustion left her cheeks pale and dark smudges under her eyes.

Even as he headed for his office, he battled the temptation to take her in his arms, settle her in his lap to warm her in his embrace. It was as if with Mia's appearance so close to the anniversary of Elizabeth's death, his brain had misfired. His emotions had entangled Mia with his memories of his beloved wife, and he was responding to this slender, dark-haired woman as if she was Elizabeth.

That had to be the reason he seemed so obsessed with her after such a short time. He usually had better sense and showed more caution.

Dawson had flown to Boston late last night, and was scheduled to meet clients this morning near MIT. Jack had met Dawson Jones fifteen years ago at Berkeley, and he'd been Jack's only true friend during the nightmare of Elizabeth's murder. Now Dawson was chief operating officer of Traynor Engineering Consulting and the public face for the business.

Dawson didn't answer his cell; no doubt he was still at lunch with the city planner of Trentville, a small town west of Boston that was looking to hire TEC for an infrastructure contract. Jack laid out the problem for Dawson in a voice-mail message; might as well give him enough information to get started on a solution.

While Jack waited for a return call, he brought up the design specs he'd planned to review this morning. After a quick read-through, his attention drifted to Mia, still curled up in the recliner. He forced his focus back to his computer, starting in on the e-mail that had accumulated during the short time he'd been gone this morning. But again his mind drifted, his awareness straying out his office door, to the slender woman in his great room.

Where the hell was Dawson? Ordinarily his friend would have checked in by now. Had Jack's voice mail gone astray? Should he call again?

Mia rose from the recliner, crossing to the pellet stove to lower the fuel feed. As he watched, she shoved her sleeves up. Lifting the hem of the sweatshirt, she flapped it away from her body to cool herself. Just the thought of how warm Mia's skin must be sent Jack's temperature rising.

She must have sensed his stare. She turned slowly, looking over her shoulder. Her lips parted and she wet them, the tip of her tongue darting briefly into view. Jack stifled a groan, setting his teeth against the heat that had settled low in his body.

The trill of the phone jolted him, sent him fumbling for the receiver. He snapped out, "Traynor," all his agitation released in the two syllables.

The pause before Dawson spoke told Jack he'd caught his friend off guard. "I wouldn't have expected the prospect of being cut off from the world by a mudslide would have set you on edge like this."

"Just came at a damned inconvenient time."

"I thought you just did your supply run yesterday."

Jack always let Dawson know when he left the house since his landline was far more reliable than the cell. Sometimes TEC's consulting business necessitated a 24/7 schedule and Dawson had to know where Jack could be contacted.

Jack didn't want to deal with the explanations Mia's presence would require. "I forgot something in town. Do you have a crew lined up to clear the slide?"

"That's what took me so long to get back to you."

Mia had disappeared from view. Jack was on his feet before he realized it, carrying the phone to the doorway to look for her. "How long will it take them?"

"I couldn't find anyone to do the work."

"With all the excavation companies in the county?" He couldn't hear her in the kitchen. Had she gone into the bathroom? "How busy could they be in the dead of winter?"

"I take it you haven't seen the news today. There was a massive slide on Highway 50—tons of rock let loose. Access between Sacramento and Carson City, Nevada, is blocked. Anyone with an earthmover, backhoe or dump truck will be tied up for the foreseeable future."

Mia returned from the hallway leading to the bathroom, Elizabeth's sweatshirt exchanged for the red Christmas sweater. The knit hugged Mia's slender curves, and the sight of her momentarily waylaid Jack's concentration. Then the significance of what Dawson had said sank in.

"You can't get anyone to clear my road?" He barked out the question.

"Not until they've got Highway 50 open. A main thoroughfare has a bit higher priority than your access road."

Mia approached, her expression wary. Jack angled away from her, lowered his voice. "I've got to get out of here."

"What did you forget in town that's so damned important?" Dawson asked.

"Nothing. I mean, it's not that important. Just…awkward."

Now Mia stood in the doorway, a tantalizing dream in red sweater and snugly fitting jeans. Jack gestured her inside and she settled in a spare office chair. She gazed out the window at the side yard.

Jack turned his back to her. "Any idea how long before a crew can be reassigned?"

"The state's talking three weeks," Dawson said, and Jack's heart sank. "But they've hired that company that's known for rush jobs to supervise. Offered a bonus for every day under twenty-one days they complete it early."

Three weeks? Jack would be a madman long before that having to face the temptation of Mia daily. Not to mention the impact of her presence during the run up to the anniversary.

"Keep working on it. Pull a crew from out of state if you need to."

"Not to distract you with the trivial," Dawson said dryly, "but the Trentville deal is looking good."

With an effort Jack switched gears as Dawson updated him on the morning's negotiations. Arranging for members of the Trentville planning commission to meet with Dawson in Boston so close to Christmas had been a major coup on his part. Several of them were heading off on vacations immediately after the meeting and would be tied up for some time after they returned. Jack felt a twinge of guilt that he'd let Mia's presence derail him so much he'd nearly forgotten his COO's mission.

Jack was grateful Dawson would be sending a detailed report in writing. With Mia only a few feet away, Jack didn't comprehend half of what Dawson said.

He set down the phone and turned his chair toward her. "There's a problem." He laid out what Dawson had told him. Mia's eyes grew wide.

"Three weeks? I can't be gone that long." The certainty in her declaration surprised him.

"Why not?"

"Because…" Her brow furrowed. "I'm supposed to be back before…"

"Before what?" Jack prodded, hoping to fan the spark of memory into flames.

She squeezed her eyes shut, her hands tightening into fists as if to grab hold of the mystery of her past. Then she let loose a gust of air, frustration clear in every line of her body.

"I don't know!" With lithe grace she jumped to her feet. "But don't you think someone must be expecting me somewhere? That someone will notice me missing?"

"I can call Dawson back, have him arrange for a few discreet inquiries—"

"No! You can't tell anyone—" She broke off, no doubt seeing the same paradox as he. She didn't want to stay with him, but she didn't want to go.

At the moment she had no choice. There was no getting around that rockslide.

She sank back into the chair, looking as fragile as she had yesterday after he'd pulled her from the creek. "I'm sorry. I'm not making any sense."

If it had been Elizabeth standing there, as needy, as overwhelmed by emotion, he'd have pulled her into his arms to soothe her. But this wasn't his late wife. And as vulnerable as Mia was, it wasn't his responsibility to be her protector. Yes, he'd keep her safe in his home until he could get her to the authorities. But beyond that, he'd have to keep firm limits in place, now that her one-night stay had extended into two to three weeks.

He couldn't let himself forget what had happened with Joanna Sanchez. The memory of that episode still burned in his gut. He'd been so sure Joanna was a second chance for him after Elizabeth's death. Except everything out of Joanna's mouth had been lies, from the false name she gave him when they first met to her seemingly heartfelt avowal of love.

Mia might be genuine, but he'd still be an idiot to let himself become involved with her as he had with Joanna. He didn't need that kind of baggage.

Her hands laced tightly in her lap. "You're a complete stranger. I don't like being trapped here with you."

"You're safe with me, Mia. I won't hurt you. I won't even touch you." Even as he said the words he wondered if he'd be able to keep that promise. "Let me at least call the sheriff's department, tell them what we know about you. Maybe they'll come up with something."

She nodded, in that moment looking so forlorn. He remembered feeling that way after Elizabeth. It would be so easy to move his chair closer to Mia's, to take her hand, pull her close. What would it hurt to comfort her?

Except it might not stop at comfort and he damn well knew it. He cursed his weakness. "It's only three weeks. I think you can survive that long."

He regretted his harsh tone the moment he said the words, even more so when she fixed him with those wounded gray eyes. Their sheen told him she barely held back tears. "I'll be sure to stay out of your way," she said, rising and hurrying from his office. A few moments later he heard the slamming of the guest-room door.

With an angry thrust of his legs, he pushed out of his chair, shoving it back against his desk. His stomach twisted with guilt.

He wasn't running a bed-and-breakfast. He didn't owe her anything but a little food and a roof over her head. She didn't mean a damn thing to him.

So why did he feel like such a bastard?

Chapter Five

Mia prowled the small space of the guest room, tears spilling from her eyes. She'd swipe them away only to have more wet her cheeks, emotions tumbling inside her like the granite and mud that had plummeted down the mountainside.

She flung herself on the bed, tried to force herself to sit still as she struggled to grab hold of a coherent thought. But the rockslide of emotions pushed her to her feet again, rioting in a dozen directions at once.

She was exploding from within with an energy she didn't even understand. She wanted desperately to get home, although she didn't remember what or where home was. Being alone with Jack terrified her, yet at the same time her imprisonment here in his isolated home gave her a sense of safety. More than anything, that feeling of security with a complete stranger agitated her, confused her.

She sat down on the edge of the bed, covering her face with her hands as she strove again to quiet her thoughts. Jack might be a stranger, but with her world out of control, he was her only thread of familiarity. Despite knowing him only a few hours, he was more concrete than any of the amorphous shadows locked away in her mind. He was a link to reality for her.

But was he more than that? If she'd been captive here with a different man, would she still feel the driving need to feel his arms around her? Would she want so badly to hold him as a shield against the enormous unknown inside her?

It isn't the man, it's the situation. She was frightened, and Jack was her only source of human contact.

And what about the sizzling attraction that zinged between them whenever he got close to her? What about the heat she felt inside when he brushed against her, the warmth that pooled low in her body when she thought of him? He might be a near-total stranger, but she couldn't deny the physical pull.

She was a young, healthy woman; he was a good-looking man. It made sense her body would respond to him. She didn't have to know anything about her former life to understand that basic biology.

She just wouldn't act on her body's urges.

At least Jack seemed honorable, had said he wouldn't touch her, harm her. Still, deep inside her, a voice told her to be suspicious of even her own judgment with him. That what she thought she knew couldn't be trusted.

Too many questions, not nearly enough answers. Frustration drove her from the bed and across the hall to the bathroom. As she splashed water on her face, she longed to wash away the doubt and confusion as easily as she did the tears and grime.

Dabbing herself dry with a hand towel, she leaned on the

vanity and stared at herself in the mirror. Her features seemed more familiar now, but only because she'd had time to study them since yesterday. Regarding herself in the mirror was like looking at someone she'd met recently. The gaze meeting hers still didn't seem like one she'd lived with for twenty-something years.

God, she wished she could find something—the color of her eyes, the shape of her nose—that would flick the switch into self-recognition. She knew Jack's face better than her own, had seen it first, the moment she'd been reborn into this frightening, baffling new world.

When she padded down the hall to the great room, she was relieved to see Jack had pulled shut his office door. But once she stood in front of the fire, pressed the buttons to lower the intensity of the flames again, she was at a loss. What did she do now?

Her gaze fell on the magazines scattered on the sofa, left there by Jack. Among the collection of reading material with esoteric, engineering-related titles she spotted two general science magazines. She plucked one of them from the slick offerings.

Her heart rate kicked higher. She turned to the table of contents, scanned it. Several articles tickled a memory. She flipped through, past photographs, charts and sidebars. She'd seen the magazine before, had read this article, had skimmed that one, she was sure of it.

The magazine clutched in her hand, she rounded the sofa and ran toward Jack's office. "Jack!"

When his door swung open, she couldn't quite stop her headlong rush. She came up against him in the doorway, palms on his chest, her body pressed against his. The magazine clattered to the floor.

She couldn't tear her eyes from his. Her heart, already beating too fast, pounded harder. As if their physical contact had strung their hearts together, the syncopation of their cadences matched. Her breathing sang alongside his, the same sensual song.

His hands had capped her shoulders, and she could feel the tension in his arms. Was he trying to pull her closer? Or push her farther away? Which did she want? Her thought processes had slowed, her primitive brain taking over, urging her to forget thinking, to act on the sensations strumming through her.

She tipped her head back, asking for…what? Her conscious self would know and would likely object, but she'd stopped listening to that part of herself. When he lowered his head, she strained up toward him, her fingers curling into his sweater, pressing against the ridge of his collarbone. Her eyes drifted shut and her body seemed to open like a flower to him.

The first stroke of his mouth against hers, and her knees went weak. She gripped him tighter, then slid her hands up around his neck for a more secure grip. The heat of his mouth burned her, tripled the pounding of her already racing heart.

When he leaned back from her, breaking the contact, she rose on the balls of her feet to keep him close. It wasn't until the tension in his arms increased that she realized he was pushing her away. The separation first felt like cold water rushing between them, then a new heat settled on her— mortification.

"I'm sorry," she said, stumbling back from him. As hot as her cheeks were, they must be blazing with color. She wished she could shrink into the floor, disappear. "That was— I shouldn't have— I don't know what—"

He stared at her, his dark eyes as deep as a starless night and just as enigmatic. She didn't know how to interpret the tautness of his jaw, the way his cheekbones stood out in sharp relief. Was he angry with the way she'd thrown herself at him? She couldn't blame him.

"Was there something you wanted?" he asked, his neutral tone convincing her the heat she'd felt had been one way only. Maybe the kiss had just been an act of curiosity on his part.

It took her a moment to recall why she'd come running to his office. "I remembered something."

Her excitement seemed so foolish now. Turning away from his steady gaze, she picked up the science magazine. With shaking hands she held it out to him. "I've read this before."

He glanced down at the magazine. "Anything else?"

"No. I just…I flipped through it and it was all familiar to me."

"Nothing that helps identify you?"

She recognized her folly then. What good did it do to remember the magazine when it got her no closer to understanding who she was? She shouldn't have gone running to him without something more concrete.

"I'm sorry. It was stupid. It was all stupid." She backed away, crumpling the magazine.

His hand on her shoulder stopped her escape. "None of this was your fault."

She forced herself to look up at him. "You're working. I shouldn't have bothered you with something so trivial."

"Not trivial. Whatever you can recall is good."

She shrugged, all too aware of how his hand shifted with

her movement. His gaze seemed to darken, impenetrable and mysterious again.

Would he say something about their kiss? Chastise her for coming on to him?

He took a step back, shoved hands into his pockets. "Anything else? I have to get back to work."

"I'm going a little stir-crazy. Do you have any books? Something to keep myself busy?"

He pushed his hair back behind his ear, impatience in the gesture. "There's a box in the garage. I'll bring them out for you."

She returned to the sofa and tidied up the magazines to give herself something to do. Jack came back a few minutes later with a good-size cardboard box, "Keepers" inscribed on one side in a feminine hand. He set the box down on the coffee table then headed back to his office without a word.

Elizabeth's, Mia guessed as she opened the flaps. The contents of the box confirmed that assumption—the majority of the books were romances, with a number of mysteries and a few biographies mixed in. Mia had no idea what kind of reading material she herself liked other than science magazines. Science fiction maybe? That genre was missing from Elizabeth's collection, but Mia was willing to try anything to keep herself occupied.

She soon found herself absorbed in a romantic suspense, only coming up for air to get herself a glass of water, then a late lunch as the day wore on. She considered asking Jack if she could make him a sandwich when she made her own, but was worried that her crazy libido might take over again. She'd suffered enough embarrassment for one day.

After lunch she got sleepy reading in front of the fire and

dozed off with the book in her lap. When she woke an hour or so later, the afghan throw had been spread across her legs.

She shoved aside the throw, and when she couldn't focus back on the novel she'd been reading, picked up a weeks-old section of the *Sacramento Bee* from a stack beside the sofa. Jack had started the crossword puzzle, still had the pen clipped to the paper. She started filling in the answers she knew, but her mind drifted and she found herself doodling in the margins. She drew eyes, fixed and staring, not Jack's enigmatic ones, but those of a stranger.

"Mia."

She rose with a start, dropping the newspaper to the sofa with a guilty flush. "I was finishing your crossword puzzle."

"I need to stretch my legs. I'm going out for a walk."

"Can I come with you?" She was wary of letting herself get too close to him, but the lure of spending time out of the house proved too much temptation.

He hesitated, then shrugged. "I'll find you a jacket."

She expected him to pull out something of his wife's, but when he returned from the coat closet, he brought her what had to be one of his own jackets. The sleeves of the rain shell hung a few inches past her fingertips. When she zipped it, she could have fit a twin of herself inside with her. But the warm fleece lining made the jacket snug and warm.

As she fumbled with the cuffs of the sleeves, Jack stepped in. "I'll do it."

He rolled the cuffs with efficient precision, the few scudding brushes of his fingertips across her skin brief and impersonal. Once he'd finished the task, the sleeves dropped neatly to her wrist bones. He started for the front door, obviously expecting her to follow.

Although the sky still glowered down at them, it had stopped raining. Excess moisture dripped from the pines and firs surrounding the house. Mist curled between the trees, hung like shawls around the tall, straight trunks.

"There's a path this way," Jack said, his voice vivid in the quiet.

The tree litter crunched under their feet as they followed the twisting trail. The wet bark of the conifers stood in stark black contrast with the bright green of the redwood needles and scalelike cedar leaves. When she tipped back her head, the water-laden branches released their moisture onto her cheeks.

As she followed behind him between the trees, her brain automatically processed her surroundings, Latin names streaming into her conscious mind. "Oh," she said softly.

Still moving, Jack turned back to her. "What?"

"Yesterday, before you found me..." She brushed her fingertips against the rough bark of a redwood. "As I walked through the forest, I knew the names of the trees—the scientific names."

Jack slowed, stopped. "Do you remember now?"

She gestured toward an incense cedar. *"Calocedrus decurrens."* She turned to point out a ponderosa pine. *"Pinus ponderosa.* The Douglas fir up ahead is *Preudotsuga menziesii."*

"Are you a botanist?"

"You'd think so, wouldn't you? But...that's not it. I just can't picture myself as a scientist."

He frowned. "But can you picture yourself anywhere?"

Under the pressure of his sharp gaze, she shook her head. He shrugged again and resumed walking."

The blankness of her mind taunted her, pricked her with

anxiety. Despite Jack's reluctance to share much about himself, she needed a diversion from her failure to remember. "Have you lived here a long time?"

His shoulders stiffened and his pace increased. She would have had to run to keep up if not for the tree that had fallen across the path. Nearly three feet in diameter, the dead cedar brought their progress to a halt.

He levered himself over the obstruction, throwing his legs over in one graceful move. Mia half wondered if he'd continue on, leaving her and her questions behind. But he put out his hand, taking hers, placing the other hand under her elbow to pull her on top of the log.

During the moments she sat on the rough bark of the cedar, she felt the dampness through her jeans, but she was barely aware of the chill. She could focus only on the feel of his hand pressed against hers. The way his dark gaze met hers, briefly traced the lines of her face.

Then he gave a tug, and she lifted her legs over with much less elegance than he'd shown. She brushed the backs of her jeans, glad his jacket had kept her from a complete soaking.

When he finally answered her question, it took her a moment to remember what she'd asked. "Three and a half years," he said as he held back a branch to allow her passage.

"You weren't living here when she died, then."

Tension stiffened his broad shoulders. He shook his head. "She died in Berkeley."

"I would have thought—" Mia paused to catch her breath as they scaled a steep climb "—you'd want to stay where you'd lived before. To preserve your memories of her."

He stopped so short Mia stumbled back trying to avoid colliding with him. She smacked her hand on the stub of a tree branch, regaining her balance.

Jack turned, his expression savage. "Why the hell would I want to remember?"

"You saved so many of her things. Her clothes, her books." Mia faltered under the fierceness of Jack's gaze. She went on in a near whisper. "To have kept so much…you must have loved her a great deal."

Jaw working, he swallowed. She didn't know if it was grief or anger that drew those sharp lines in his face. Maybe a little of both.

"I loved her more than you can imagine."

Swinging around, he started back up the hill, setting a pace so rapid that Mia fell behind. As the trees thinned into a clearing, she could keep him in view, saw him stop beside a granite boulder, lean against it.

When she reached the massive boulder, Jack moved over a bit to give her space alongside him. She kept a few inches between them when she took her place. Although she couldn't feel the heat of his body through her jacket and sweater, she could all too clearly imagine it.

His arms crossed over his chest, Jack stared across down at the trees below. A few blackened redwood trunks dotted the clearing; other smaller trees had toppled across the hillside. The ragged tops of the snags still standing gave witness to a trial by fire. Whitethorn, deerbrush and green leaf manzanita filled the space between the dead trees, grudgingly ceding space to white and red fir seedlings just beginning to show above the level of the brush.

"How long ago since it burned?" Mia looked around her, judging the height of the firs. "Ten, fifteen years?"

Jack raised a brow. "Twelve and a half years ago. We were in escrow. Nearly fifty acres burned, three of them on my property. How on earth could you have known that?"

"From the amount and type of growth." She swept an arm across the landscape. "The brush comes back almost immediately. Although the wind blows in tree seeds, the whitethorn and deerbrush shades them and slows their growth. The only reason the red and white fir have done as well as they have is that they're shade tolerant."

Jack gave her a bemused smile. "You're a walking textbook."

"At least I'm remembering *something*." She pointed out the twisted red branches of a manzanita. "That variety both sprouts from its burl—its root—and grows from seed. In fact, the fire has to scarify the seed for it to grow."

Somehow they'd edged toward each other, his shoulder pressing against hers. She would have thought he'd move away again, break the contact, but instead he dropped his arms so that the back of his hand brushed against her. Now she didn't have to imagine the body heat radiating from him. Unlike before when he rolled up her sleeves, he moved his hand toward her with intention. His fingers wrapped around hers, the pressure of them slight but definite.

He made no other move toward her. He still looked away, off across the regenerated landscape. She could only see his jaw, the high cheekbone. She wanted those dark eyes turned toward her. As opaque as they so often were, she might be able to see something in them that would help her understand what was going on.

Heat curled up her arm, hot as flame. Was this what the forest felt as wildfire rushed through it? Like the manzanita, whose seeds needed to be seared for rebirth, would she be reborn through Jack's fire? If she couldn't be herself again, could she be someone new?

"This is what I miss the most," he said, his voice low in Mia's ear. "Holding her hand. Her palm against mine."

Now empathy tangled with the sensuality he'd stirred within her. She tried to muster a response, to say something that would soothe him. But the touch of his fingers laced with hers drove coherence from her mind.

"We'd sit together, on the sofa or in bed at night. We'd be reading or watching television. She'd reach across, take my hand." His fingers gripped Mia's convulsively, as if he groped for his dead wife. "Sometimes I think if I could just hold her hand one more time…"

He pushed away from the boulder, shoving his hands into his pockets. "I need to get back. Still have a few things to finish before dinner."

He waited until she fell in behind him, then started back down the trail. The going was easier downhill, although in the oversize shoes the slick mud made the footing treacherous. She slipped twice, biting back a gasp each time, regaining her balance on her own by reaching for a redwood trunk. Jack moved on ahead of her, apparently unaware of her predicament.

Then her heel caught on a protruding rock as she slid, inertia all but launching her forward. Her flailing hands found nothing within reach to grab, and she couldn't hold back a cry of fear.

She landed, not on the rock-studded hillside but in Jack's arms. He took a step back to absorb the energy of her fall, then held her tight until she could get her feet under her. Once she'd centered herself again, he let go.

"Thank you." She smiled, still shaky from the near disaster. "That was a lucky catch."

"I was watching you," he said, his expression serious. "I wouldn't have let you fall."

Of course he wouldn't. She knew so little about him, but she felt secure in that knowledge. No matter what, Jack would keep her safe.

Chapter Six

He'd been shut up in his office for two hours since he and Mia returned from their walk and had accomplished nearly nothing in that time. The engineering report he should have completed by this afternoon was still unfinished. The spreadsheet he'd promised to e-mail to Dawson so he'd have it when he returned from Boston mocked Jack on his computer screen, a third of the data unentered, the final calculations still undone.

His gaze strayed to the closed door. He should have left it open, kept an eye on Mia while he worked. Although her memory loss seemed to be the only lasting effect of her ordeal in the creek, he couldn't be sure she wouldn't lose consciousness again.

But he'd felt too vulnerable, too stripped bare by her. He knew it had nothing to do with Mia, that his emotions were always harder to control as the calendar marched closer to the anniversary date. Even still, her presence had brought all the loneliness and grief out in sharp relief.

Why else would he have taken her hand like that up on the hillside? Spilled his guts to her? No doubt he'd embarrassed her. He felt like a complete ass.

Restlessness drove him to his feet. He would have to finish the spreadsheet and report this evening. It would give him something to do besides obsess over Mia.

Swinging the door open, he scanned the great room for her. The back of the sofa blocked his view; he couldn't see if she lay there reading or napping. The pellet stove still burned on low, and the evening chill curled toward him through the large space.

He remembered the wave of coolness when he'd opened the door of his and Elizabeth's Berkeley apartment that night. They would leave the thermostat down low when they weren't there. The first one home would raise the temperature so the furnace would cycle on. The chill when he'd entered that December day had given him his first inkling that something was amiss. That and the silence when he called Elizabeth's name.

In those first few moments before he'd found her bloody and broken, he'd tried to fool himself into thinking everything was okay. She'd just stepped out briefly and had forgotten to lock the door behind her. If he just shut his eyes and waited, she'd return.

Then he'd stepped into the kitchen and found the body of his murdered wife. His world had ended the instant he saw her, still and lifeless on the floor. Even as he held her, shouted her name, he'd known it was over.

When they arrested him three weeks later, he could hardly bring himself to care, despite his innocence. Elizabeth was dead. What did it matter where he finished his days—in San Quentin or in the prison of his own unending loss?

The fragrance of sautéed onions brought him back to the present, telling him Mia must be in the kitchen starting dinner. Competing forces warred within him—the urge to see her, the reluctance to let himself be stripped bare by this intriguing woman. Elizabeth, as a professor of abnormal psychology, could have offered up some complex phobia or psychological condition to explain what he was feeling.

They'd had an agreement during their marriage: he wouldn't bore her with the technical specs of flood catch-basin construction and she wouldn't psychoanalyze him. Right now, though, he felt as if he needed his head examined.

To delay the inevitable, he took a side trip to the garage for more stove pellets. Hefting the forty pounder back inside, he cut a corner from the plastic bag and poured pellets into the near-empty hopper. As he shook the last of them into the stove, he glanced into the kitchen where Mia stood at the cooktop.

Adjusting the pellet stove to a higher heat, he crumpled the empty bag and headed into the kitchen. Mia looked back over her shoulder at him as he stuffed the bag into the trash. Her brief smile stopped him in his tracks, literally froze him there with his hand still on the trash-can lid. When she turned back to the stove, he shook himself and, freed of her spell, he went to wash his hands.

As the water rinsed away the soap, another flashback intruded—him sobbing as he cleaned Elizabeth's blood from his hands. He slammed shut the water and the memory, angry that he'd let the ugliness into his mind with Mia there. Yes, it was December, the time of year when his exertion of even the most powerful will couldn't keep the images at bay. But he'd made a point over the years of only allowing himself to lose control when he was alone.

And then it hit him hard—he wouldn't be alone for the anniversary this year. Mia would be here, would see every moment his self-control chipped away, would see what he became. If he'd felt exposed earlier today, it would be nothing to the nakedness he would reveal.

Except he wouldn't let her see. He damn well wouldn't. He wrapped his fingers around the edge of the sink, the corner of the granite countertop digging into his hand. It was time he stopped indulging himself, anyway. Five years was long enough.

"Are you hungry?"

Jack jumped, unaware that she'd moved up behind him. He turned toward her, forcing a smile on his face that must have looked like a grimace. "I could eat." His stomach knotted at the thought.

She studied his face, her gray eyes so soft, the curve of her mouth so sweet, his heart ached. He wanted desperately to pull her into his arms, to feel her slender body against his. To feel the warmth of her.

He edged away. "I'll set the table."

He laid out plates and flatware in the dining room, then carried in from the kitchen a basket of fragrant biscuits. Mia brought out a bowl of canned peaches, then a covered dish that she set on a trivet.

"I hope you don't mind me taking over your kitchen," she said as he pulled out her chair for her.

"No problem." Except it was. It brought back too many memories of returning home to a warm apartment, to Elizabeth putting out dinner for them.

A tantalizing aroma rose when she opened the covered dish. "Sausage and onions in a honey-mustard sauce. I found the recipe in one of your cookbooks."

He served them each a portion. In spite of himself, his mouth watered at the delectable smell. "You haven't forgotten how to cook."

"That's strange, isn't it? What I remember and what I don't." She took a biscuit from the basket, then offered him one. "I didn't need a recipe for these. My hands just seemed to know what to do."

He glanced down at those small, clever hands and let himself imagine what else they could do. If he thought about her body, her mouth, how her skin would feel under his fingertips, how it would taste, then he could push aside his more dangerous emotions. He didn't have to act on his sexual fantasies, but he could use them as a buttress to hold himself together.

It wasn't hard to think of Mia that way. To imagine pulling her into his lap even now, to push up that sweater, feel the narrowness of her waist, the shape of her back as he moved his hand higher. He could taste that curve of her throat, see if it was as sweet as the honey she was licking from her fingers.

She lifted her gaze to his, one finger still in her mouth. Sensation shot low in his body, and he grew hard just watching the color rise in her cheeks. Even when she lowered her hand to her lap, dropped her gaze to her plate, heat surged through him, goading him. The handle of the fork in his hand bit into his skin, his grip so tight on it he was probably bending the metal.

But despite the way his body screamed in frustration, this physical response to her was better than the grief, the rage. He had enough willpower to keep his hands off Mia. He didn't have the strength to fight the black emotions that threatened to ambush his soul, wash him away the way the creek nearly had Mia.

He shifted in his seat, his erection pushing on the placket

of his jeans. The table kept Mia from seeing, although he couldn't quite guard his face. Her sidelong glances told him she saw desire there, must have known that he wanted her. He edged away, keeping his focus on his dinner. He didn't want her to be afraid of him.

She sure knew her way around a kitchen. The biscuits melted in his mouth, the sweet-savory sausage and onion had him leaning back in his chair, eyes closed to appreciate the layers of flavor. Elizabeth had been a hazard around pots and pans, her culinary disasters far outnumbering her successes. She laughingly would tell him she had two favorite dishes— takeout and anything he cooked for her.

By the time they cleared the table, Jack had himself under control, his mind directed to the tasks he had to complete before tomorrow. He helped Mia bring in the few dishes they'd used, put away leftovers while she loaded the dishwasher. He was all but patting himself on the back at the way he'd leashed his impulses, had kept his head on straight while he worked with Mia tidying up the kitchen.

He wasn't sure how it happened. She was wiping down the granite countertop and he was reaching around her to stow a serving bowl on an upper shelf. She turned just as he leaned in toward the counter. Her slender body curved into his, the wet cloth in her hand dropping to the floor.

He should have backed away. But the heat rekindled instantly inside him, keeping him fixed in place, his hands covering hers on his chest. Without even thinking, he tugged her even closer, hand at the small of her back, pulling her hips into his.

His erection pressed into the softness of her belly. Her eyes wide, her fingers curled into his sweater, and he thought she would push back, twist away. It would have been better to stop this before it started. But instead she wound her arms around him, bringing him even closer.

"Mia," he said, her whispered name a warning, a supplication. He didn't seem to have any sense left; he prayed she did. But she stretched taller, tipping her head back, her lips parting. There was a roaring in his ears, like the sound of the swollen creek, wild and reckless, overflowing its bank.

He never should have let it get this far. Because if he kissed her, he feared it wouldn't stop at that. That he wouldn't let her go again until he had her in his bed, her naked body under his. And that would be insanity—he'd only met her yesterday. When he'd wanted nothing to do with women these past few years, why suddenly had this one so quickly stripped him bare?

He brushed his mouth against hers, the lightest touch. He wouldn't let it go any further than that. Wouldn't run his tongue along that silken lower lip, wouldn't dip just inside for a first taste. Even though his body felt as if it would explode if he didn't press inside her soon—now. He would hold back.

Her tongue, tentative, searching, was his undoing. He felt the wet tip of it graze the corner of his mouth before it retreated. He couldn't suppress a groan that shuddered through his body. He was lost now, beyond caring about consequences.

He turned her, lifting her to the countertop, spreading her legs so he could stand between them. His hands slipped from her waist to her hips, his thumbs stretching toward the cleft of her thighs. He wanted to reach inside her jeans and feel the dampness. Then he would put his mouth there and push her over the edge.

Overlaying the pounding of his heart, the ringing of his office phone snagged one small corner of his focus. He didn't give a damn about whoever was calling, had no intention of hurrying to his office to answer the phone. But it was enough to inject a grain of sanity into his brain. Enough to persuade him to pause, to reconsider.

His gaze locked with hers. If he'd seen only the heat he'd seen a few moments earlier, he would have continued, done all the things to her that his fertile imagination had laid out. But behind the desire in those compelling gray eyes, a trace of doubt had bloomed. She might be nine-tenths ready for him, but it was the one-tenth that mattered.

The phone had stopped ringing, rolling over to voice mail. If it was Dawson, he'd try the cell next. Jack would be ready to answer it.

With her arm around him, Jack helped Mia scoot down from the counter. He turned away to adjust his jeans, then started toward his office, grabbing up his cell phone from the dining-room table. A savage impulse to throw the palm-size piece of electronics across the great room welled up inside him, but he just gripped the phone harder. He didn't dare look back at Mia. If there was embarassment in her face, he wouldn't be able to stand the guilt. If it was unresolved passion, it was better he didn't know.

The cell trilled just as Jack stepped over the threshold of his office, the caller ID telling him it was Dawson. He took a long breath, lowering himself into his chair before he answered.

"Hey, what's up?" The informal greeting sounded stiff to his own ears.

"Three-hour delay in Denver. Thought I'd never get home." Dawson's heavy sigh revealed his exhaustion. "Just downloaded e-mail and didn't see that spreadsheet. Didn't know if it got caught in my spam filter."

"I haven't sent it yet. Still had to check a few figures." Out of the corner of his eye, he saw Mia move through the great room. He swung the door shut. "I'll get it to you within the hour."

"As long as I've got it by morning for the weekly status meeting."

The oak office door might as well have not been there. He could so easily imagine Mia curled on the sofa, the firelight edging her dark hair with gold.

With an effort he pulled his attention back to Dawson. "Any progress on finding a work crew?"

"No interest from anyone out of state to take on a job that small, even with a pay incentive. Hate to say it, but you'll just have to wait it out."

He hadn't expected anything different. He'd seen the articles on various news sites earlier in the day, saw the extent of the disaster on Highway 50. Several homes had been destroyed, taken out by the hillside's fall. His road blockage was trivial by comparison.

Jack's gaze strayed to the home page on his computer screen. While checking the news that morning, he'd also scanned for anything that might identify Mia. Not an in-depth search—he'd promised her he wouldn't dig around. But there was a way to set Dawson, a confessed Internet-news junkie, on Mia's trail without breaking that promise.

Pitching his voice lower, Jack asked, "Have you heard anything about that missing woman?"

Dawson yawned in Jack's ear. "What missing woman?"

"A young woman, maybe late twenties. Saw something about it on the Web. She went missing yesterday."

"I was in meetings all day yesterday. Incommunicado

most of today. I haven't heard a thing. What Web site did you see it on?"

"I can't remember now. Just wondering if you'd heard an update about her."

Dawson couldn't quite stifle a second yawn. "I could do a search for you. You have a name?"

"Mia something." Guilt twinged inside him that he'd told Dawson that much. "Get to bed. I want you awake for tomorrow's status meeting."

After they said their goodbyes, Jack set the cell beside his monitor. He'd at least planted the seed with his friend. As busy as Dawson was, he'd watch for stories about missing women, would likely find mention of Mia's disappearance long before Jack would.

By the time he finished the spreadsheet and the calculations for the engineering report, his eyes were burning and his shoulders ached. He rose, trying to stretch out the kinks in his cramped body, wincing when he saw the time. Nearly 1:00 a.m. The status meeting started at seven-thirty and there was still an hour more of prep work he needed to do. He'd have to get up early, finish it then.

At least Mia was already asleep, out of temptation's way. He cracked open his office door and flipped off the light at the same time. The small lamp on the end table and the yellow-orange glow of flames in the pellet stove were the only illumination in the great room.

Rubbing his eyes, Jack made his way to the stove and shut off the pellet feed. As he passed in front of the sofa, his feet caught on something—the shoes he'd loaned Mia. When he bent to set them out of the way, he saw her.

Her head cushioned by a pillow she must have borrowed

from the guest room, she lay stretched out on the sofa. A book was splayed spine up on her stomach, her thumb hooked between the pages as a bookmark. He imagined her setting the book down, maybe intending to just close her eyes for a few moments. But from the deep, regular sound of her breathing, she'd been asleep for some time.

Red orange spilled from the dying flames of the stove, mixing with the white glow of the lamplight. She would have been beautiful in any light, but the dimness of the room added a mystery to her face. He wanted to rest his hand on her cheek, feel her breath curling against his wrist. Listen to every soft inhalation.

How many times had he watched Elizabeth sleep? Not enough. He would have done it far more often if he'd known how little time they would have together. He would have dedicated his life to watching her.

Jack snapped off the lamp, then dropped to his knees and sat cross-legged beside the sofa. Mia's free hand lay uncurled, relaxed beside her body. Moving slowly, Jack rested his hand lightly in hers. He leaned his head against Mia's leg and gazed up into her face.

Just for a few minutes. Then he'd carry her to her room so she'd be more comfortable. So she wouldn't be frightened if she woke in the night.

But for the moment he would drink her in. Watch her chest rise and fall, feel the warmth of her against his hand. Appreciate this woman, this stranger. As he would Elizabeth if he could have.

He kept his gaze on Mia until the last of the fire died away and darkness cloaked the room.

Chapter Seven

When Mia opened her eyes and looked around her at the milky light seeping through the blinds, the first thing she noticed was the utter silence. No wind, no raindrops falling on the roof, no dripping from the trees. Just cotton-wool silence.

As she rose, pushed aside the thick comforter, she remembered. She'd fallen asleep on the sofa, reading in front of the fire. Despite the romantic-suspense novel's riveting climax, she'd drifted off. And Jack had brought her here.

At least he hadn't undressed her as he had the first day. She'd thrown away enough of her dignity last night when she'd all but begged him to kiss her. He'd responded— there was no mistaking that thick ridge of flesh he'd pressed against her. But thank God he'd had enough chivalry to pull back. If he'd taken advantage of her lack of self-control, they might have woken up in bed together, and she wouldn't still be wearing her blue jeans and sweater.

Just as she wondered how she could wear the same grungy clothes another day, she noticed the stacks on the dresser. She expected the same baggy sweat suits Jack had offered her before. Instead she found jeans and sweaters only one size larger than her own size. He'd unearthed a worn pair of slippers and another pack of panties, as well.

Grabbing up a change of clothes, she hurried across the hall to the bathroom, one eye cast toward Jack's office. She wasn't keen to confront him yet this morning. A shower and fresh clothes would make the awkwardness easier to bear.

And awkward it would be. She was determined to talk to him about what nearly happened last night, make it clear that whatever subconscious impulses from her former life might be driving her, she intended to resist them. If her behavior of the past few days was any indication, she was apparently a promiscuous woman. The thought made her squirm with embarrassment, but she had to accept the possibility.

When she stepped out into the great room, feeling blessedly fresh and clean, the view out the large front window derailed her thoughts. Snow blanketed the woods outside, clumped on the branches of the cedars and redwoods. Fat flakes continued to fall, at times so thick they obscured the trees behind them.

That explained the silence. She crossed to the window, mesmerized by the white-on-white landscape. As she stared at the dizzying fall of snowflakes, she was struck by the newness of it all. She'd never seen this before, not face-to-face, anyway. She would have seen photos, movies with scenes of snowfall. But she'd never watched the real thing.

She wanted to go out in it, to gather it up in her hands and feel the iciness of it. Pat it into a ball and throw it at a tree, make a snowman, a snow angel. Let the flakes fall on her tongue and decorate her hair.

Rapt, she barely heard Jack's office door open. She looked over her shoulder at him, smiling, filled with joy. He moved toward her, stripping off his headset and shoving it in a back pocket.

"You found the clothes." His voice was rough with exhaustion.

"Thanks. They do fit better."

"Found one last bag of Elizabeth's things out in the shed. She didn't wear those much. She went on a crazy diet one year, dropped thirty pounds." He yawned. "She was too skinny."

"Like me," Mia said, hands falling to bony hips.

"You're the right size for you. Maybe a little too thin."

She was suddenly aware of how close he was standing. Her gaze dropped to his hands, large and capable, then drifted up his muscular forearms. He'd shoved the sleeves of his black sweater up, and her fingers itched to stroke him from wrist to elbow.

Impatient with herself, with the way her thoughts seemed beyond her control, she edged away from him. "I've never seen it snow before."

"Then you're from somewhere it doesn't snow."

"I guess so. That doesn't exactly narrow things down much." She spread a hand on the window glass. "It's beautiful."

"It is," he said softly. But when she glanced over at him, he was staring at her, not at the winter storm.

"I'd like to go out. See what it's like."

She thought he'd tell her no. Instead he pulled the headset from his pocket and tossed it on the window seat. "I have some old ski overalls we can make work for you. No boots, so we can't stay out for long."

The overalls swam on her, the legs sagging around her ankles. He made her pull on two more pairs of socks, then the oversize shoes. Gloves tucked in the zippered pocket of the bib would keep her hands warm, a wool hat covered her head.

He wouldn't let her go beyond the gravel drive, obliterated beneath a foot of snow. But she could tip her head back and snag snowflakes on her tongue, could pack together enough of the lacy white stuff to make a credible snowball. Her throw fell short of the nearest tree, the ball poking a hole in the soft drift piled below it.

Jack watched her from the front of the garage, a bemused smile on his face. It was the most relaxed she'd seen him since she'd first woken to find him standing over her. It seemed she was getting a glimpse of the man he used to be, when Elizabeth was still alive.

Her heart ached at the thought of being loved so powerfully by a man. Had she felt that kind of love? Was there a man in her life, someone who, even now, desperately sought her, would give anything to have her back with him?

A love that strong—wouldn't she feel it even now, despite the loss of memories? Wouldn't that love be lodged so deeply in her heart it would be as much a part of her as her own breath? A brilliant light that couldn't be dimmed or forgotten?

But as she struggled to remember, it wasn't light that glimmered in the back of her mind, but something dark, something edged with fear. Her heart hammered violently in her chest as an iciness that had nothing to do with the snow overcame her.

The air was suddenly too cold to breathe. Her fingers, still warm in the heavy gloves, spasmed as if to ward off something frightful. Alarm bloomed inside her, building into terror.

Jack's gaze narrowed on her. "We should go in."

Her teeth were chattering now, as if she were chilled from deep within. She hurried past him, arms wrapped around herself. The fear seemed to nip at her heels, impelling her toward the safety of the house.

She kicked off the wet shoes and peeled off the overalls in the tiled foyer, her hands shaking despite the warmth indoors. She tried to convince herself it was just the cold that had sent shudders through her. But even when she pushed off the damp socks and thrust her feet into the slippers, even when she moved to the stove to stand inches from the roaring flames, her body still shook.

Jack threw the afghan around her shoulders. Then, when she still trembled, he wrapped his arms around her and pulled her close to the blast furnace of his body. As flashes of fear jabbed at her, clutched at her heart, she burrowed even deeper into his embrace. She wondered how one man could generate so much heat, could melt away the knot of dread inside her.

Finally her body relaxed and she felt too hot to stand so close to the fire. She tugged away, wary of the sensual response that she risked with Jack's nearness. Keeping her eyes downcast, not yet ready to see what might be in his face, she huddled on the sofa, the afghan draped around her.

He sat opposite her on the sofa. She could feel his gaze on her. "That wasn't just the cold," she told him, her fingers pleating the crocheted throw.

"I didn't think so."

"I had a—" she tried to think of an innocuous label to place on the blackness that had crouched inside her "—a flashback."

"What did you see?" he asked.

"Nothing. It was more what I felt." She tried to get a handle on the fear, but in the warm, well-lit house, it seemed to have dissipated. "Afraid," she said finally, irritated at the inadequacy of the word. "Just out of the blue."

"Any idea what set it off?"

Something in his tone lifted her gaze to his and she saw the intensity in his eyes. Could he possibly know she was thinking about him, about the love he'd felt for his wife? Surely not. And she wasn't about to reveal her thoughts to him.

"I was enjoying myself in the snow. Wondering if there's...anyone missing me, worried about where I am." She stretched her mouth into a stiff smile. "Trying to psychoanalyze me?"

"Elizabeth was the psychologist, not me." He shifted on the sofa, rubbed a hand on the back of his neck, crossed and uncrossed his legs. "Listen, about last night—"

"I won't do that again," she blurted out.

He turned toward her, surprise in his face. "Do what again?"

Heat burned her cheeks. "Push myself on you. Come on to you that way."

He stared for a long, uncomfortable beat. "I think you've got it backward."

"In that other life, the one I can't remember...I must be more...casual about sex." She said the last word in a whisper. "Less discriminating about men."

He raised one brow. "So you would have wanted to kiss any man. I just happened to be handy."

"Yes. No." She covered her flushed face with her hands. "I don't know. I don't know how else to explain it. I'm not usually that way."

The truth of that statement settled inside her. She dropped her hands. "I'm not. I don't know why I—"

"You didn't. You've got it backward," he said again, then rose. "I'm late for my eleven-o'clock call."

As he started around the end of the sofa, his gaze fell on the stack of magazines on the table. He picked up the newspaper with the crossword puzzle.

"Sorry, I've nearly finished it," Mia told him.

"No problem." He turned the newspaper sideways and studied the eyes she'd drawn all around the margin of the page. "You drew these?" At her nod, he dropped the newspaper and strode from the room.

Not to his office as she expected, but down the hall to his bedroom. A few minutes later, he returned with a large art pad and plastic case.

He set them down beside her on the sofa. "I tried this after Elizabeth was…after she died." He gave her a self-deprecating laugh. "Art therapy. Unfortunately, I can't draw a straight line. Maybe you can get some use out of it."

He turned away, making a side trip to the window seat for the headset. A moment later he'd closed himself in his office.

The eyes she'd doodled on the newspaper stared up at her, as enigmatic as her sudden fear this morning. She'd assumed they'd meant nothing, had just been idle scribbling while she tried to answer twenty-two down or eighteen across. But maybe there was more of a message in the seemingly random drawings.

Flipping to a fresh page on the pad, she opened the black plastic case and chose a pencil.

Through sheer force of will Jack got through the rest of his workday. He didn't stop for lunch, grabbing a slapped-together sandwich around two, then wolfing down the dinner Mia prepared. He thanked her for cooking, ordered her out of the kitchen so he could clean up on his own, then returned to his office for another few hours.

His only prayer for keeping Mia out of his mind was to fill it with something else. He'd used that trick often enough over the years to battle his grief, to hold at bay the horror film loop of Elizabeth's bloody body lying in the kitchen at the apartment. With the days moving inexorably toward the anniversary, he'd have a double whammy to contend with. But he'd have to find a way to handle the emotional overload, to keep his annual implosion private. He had no other choice.

When he went out to shut off the pellet stove, a part of him longed to find her there again, sleeping. The sofa was empty. She must have taken the drawing pad with her to her room; it and the pencil case were gone. He hoped it did her more good than it had done him.

He'd lied to her. Although he wasn't much of an artist, he could draw more than a straight line. But the images he'd sketched had sickened him, full of violence and cruelty. His crude drawings depicted all the things he'd like to do to Elizabeth's murderer, opened a side of him that had frightened him. Even Elizabeth's former colleague, who had recommended the art therapy, agreed it was doing him more harm than good. So he'd burned the drawings and hadn't picked up pad or pencil since.

He fell asleep the instant his head hit the pillow, woke abruptly before the alarm went off. Directed himself through another day of grueling work, aching for the sight of Mia, for one touch of her hand. Stared out the window at the endless fall of snow as it piled up, drifts nearly to the bottom of the window.

If the sudden cold front that had brought the snow lingered even after precipitation ceased, that blanket of white could be around a long time. It was likely complicating the removal of rock and mud on Highway 50, slowing down the process. That didn't bode well for getting his own road cleared.

He caught glimpses of Mia when he emerged from his office for more coffee or for a bathroom break. She'd be in the window seat with the art pad or curled up on the sofa with a book. That night when he finally marched himself to bed, so exhausted he staggered, he nearly collided with her in the hallway. He didn't touch her, made a point of stepping well clear of her. But her nearness kicked his body into high gear again, slapping aside his tiredness. It took him two restless hours to fall asleep.

The next morning he woke at 6:00 a.m. with a sense of inexplicable doom. As he stared at the date on the digital clock—Wednesday, December 17—his body started shaking. The seventeenth had been a Wednesday five years ago. He'd kissed Elizabeth goodbye that morning, had driven to SFO to catch a nine-o'clock flight to Seattle. When he returned seven days later, he found her dead on the kitchen floor.

Get a grip, he told himself, dragging himself out of bed. It was just that he was running on fumes, fighting his libido at the same time he dealt with the anniversary. He'd indulged himself for too long, taking advantage of his usual isolation to let go of his self-control.

The smell of fresh-brewed coffee as he paced down the hall told him he wouldn't be the first one in the kitchen. The spicy muffins he saw cooling on a rack meant Mia had gotten up long before him. She sat on a stool at the breakfast bar, cup of black coffee in her hands, a few muffin crumbs on the plate beside her. The art pad sat closed on the dining-room table.

Her cheeks had filled out some even in the few days she'd been there. Her skin, still pale, had bloomed with faint color. The bruises on her face, after purpling a day after he'd rescued her, had started to fade. From her pushed-up sleeves, he could see she'd removed the dressing on her left arm and the scratch was healing nicely.

He wanted to sit beside her, to wrap an arm around her, nestle her head in the crook of his neck. Breathe in the scent of her hair, feel its silk on her cheek. Hook his fingers in hers, feel her pulse against his thumb.

He just wanted her close, and it had nothing to do with sex.

He turned his back on her, pulling down a mug. "Good morning."

She glanced up at him, then fiddled with the crumbs on her plate, swiping them up with a finger. When she licked them off, he felt the surge low in his body and welcomed the sexual response. Better that than the longing that made him feel so vulnerable.

But then he saw the haunted look in her eyes, the trace of fear. He tugged a stool around opposite her, then sat with his coffee and muffin. "What's wrong?"

Hands wrapped around her steaming cup, she took a sip. "Dreams."

"Nightmares?"

She swallowed convulsively. "Some of them. But nothing I could describe. Nothing that makes sense."

"And the rest of them?"

"I see myself. As a child. At a park with my mother and

father. At least, I'm guessing that's who they are." She shook her head. "None of it's clear enough to understand."

"What do they look like?"

"Nothing like me," she said, frustration clear in her tone. "The mother in my dream is blond. My father has light brown hair. Both of them are short and plump. For all I know, they're just figments of my imagination."

"Maybe you're adopted."

Something flickered in her eyes, a light of recognition. "Maybe," she said thoughtfully. "But how does that help me? They're just two faces from my dreams. No names, nothing to place them."

She looked so lost, it took everything in him not to reach across the counter and take her hand. Instead he picked up the muffin and bit into it. It was sweet and warm, with chunks of apples and a hint of cinnamon. Cinnamon-sugar crusted the top.

"Whatever else you are, you're a hell of a baker."

"Butcher, baker, candlestick maker," she recited. "Which one am I?"

He had no answer for her. "Any luck with the drawing?"

"You tell me." Swiveling on her stool, she grabbed the pad from the table. He shifted aside her coffee cup and plate so she could set the pad on the granite countertop.

She opened it to the first page. The accuracy of the pencil drawing startled him. She'd sketched the line of redwoods visible out the front window, capturing the rough texture of the bark, the complexity of the graceful, needled branches. She'd even drawn in the rocks and deadfall beneath the trees.

"You're an artist." He flipped to the next sketch, a snow scene with afternoon shadows of cedars criss-crossing, blue gray on the blanket of white.

"You would think so." She turned to a third page, a study of his mantel with the pellet stove bright with flame. "It was almost as if it wasn't my hand doing the drawing." She spread her fingers over the paper. "But it doesn't seem right. I have talent, but I'm not an artist. I think this is just something I do."

"Have you tried to draw something that isn't right in front of you? Like those eyes?"

She shuddered. "I was going to try that today. But I'm afraid."

She shut the pad, then carried her cup and plate to the sink. She seemed to almost be sleepwalking as she left the kitchen.

The day passed as the previous one had, with Jack driving himself as hard as he could, to forget about Mia. At the same time he struggled to push from his conscious mind the minute-by-minute memories from five years ago.

When he joined Mia for a late dinner, he didn't like the pinched look around her mouth, the way she avoided meeting his gaze. It was as if she was fragmenting, and fighting to keep herself in one piece.

He didn't trust the urgency to pull her into his arms. Would it be to comfort her, to help her hold it together? Or was it just an excuse to feel her close to him? As off-kilter as his life was, did he really have anything to give her?

She went to bed shortly after dinner, letting him clean up without complaint. He interrupted his work twice to check on her, the sight of her sound asleep easing his worry.

He'd just turned off the lights in his office, looking forward to climbing into bed when he heard her moan. He took off running, reaching her room just as she screamed.

"No! Stop it, no! Don't—"

He touched her arm, the lightest pressure, and her eyes

snapped open. She wrenched herself away from him, scrambling to the other side of the bed. "Leave me alone!"

Her chest heaved as she gasped for breath. The pale light from the hallway showed him the terror in her eyes. He was nothing but a dark shadow to her in the dim room.

He clicked on the bedside lamp. "It's just me, Mia."

Her fingers curled tightly in the comforter. The terror melted from her face as she recognized him. Tears filled her eyes and she reached across the bed. "Please," she whispered.

Only a monster would have refused her. He sat beside her on the bed and pulled her into his arms.

Chapter Eight

Even lying on top of the blankets fully dressed, Jack responded to the woman curved tightly against him. Images flooded his mind: stripping off his clothes, slipping under the covers with her, peeling away the too-large pajamas. Feeling her, skin to skin, a sensory overload his body craved.

He just let the fantasies play out as he stayed right where he was, Mia in his arms. One small hand held tight to his waist, the other curled at his shoulder. He could dip his head down, press a kiss into her palm, rest his cheek against her fingers.

He heard only her steady breathing and he thought she'd drifted off to sleep again. But then she stirred against him. Eyes still closed, she murmured, "How do I make it stop?"

"You can't." He stroked her arm. "You shouldn't. You have to remember."

"There's something in the way. I mean…" Her eyes

squeezed shut more tightly. "Something I have to pass through before I can get to the memories. Something…horrible."

"An accident?" he asked. "I really think your car is wrecked somewhere on my road. Somewhere farther down, past the slide."

"Maybe." She scrunched her face. "Can you turn off the light?"

He pressed the switch. The near darkness felt far too intimate. But he was here for Mia, not to satisfy his body's urgings.

"The thing is," she continued, "I have no memory of a crash. The little I can recall of recent events, I was walking *across* the mountainside, not up it. I stumbled upon the road not far from where you found me. On *this* side of the rockslide."

"It's still possible you blanked that part—the accident, climbing the hill."

"But why?" she asked. She looked up at him, her gray eyes dark in the semilight. "It's not as if I had a traumatic brain injury. I was unconscious a few minutes, not in a coma. Why would my mind have wiped it out if it was something as simple as a car accident?"

"I don't know." He fitted his arm more snugly around her. "You should get under the covers."

"No. I shouldn't."

"I'll be fine." She sighed. "Go to bed."

"After you fall asleep."

"Won't help." She slurred her words, tiredness overcoming her. "They're waiting."

Minutes later she was asleep, her breathing steady, her body lax in his arms. He wanted so damn much to stay here with her. It was far too easy to tell himself it would be for her benefit, not his. But with her asleep, the only one comforted by his being in her bed was him.

He pulled free of her, made sure she didn't wake. Then he padded softly from her room to his own.

Hoping an arcane engineering publication would put him to sleep, he read until his eyes burned, then turned off the light. As he lay there, too restless to sleep, he heard Mia moan twice, cry out once. Not a scream, just a soft plea. Then she quieted and he finally drifted off to sleep himself.

The next morning a soft rap on his office door drew Jack's attention from his conference call. Swinging open the door, he gestured Mia inside, his voice faltering only briefly as he spoke to Dawson and the design team. If anyone noticed, they would likely put it down to the extended hours he'd been working.

He pointed to the extra chair, then turned his back on Mia. Her fragrance was like an irresistible mist. After last night, the temptation to reach for her, pull her close had increased tenfold. He'd have to fight to keep his mind on his work.

Five minutes later, everyone but Dawson had signed off. After discussing a few last details on an in-progress request for proposal, Dawson switched gears. "How are you holding up?"

Jack could have pretended his friend was referring to the weather or the mudslide blocking his road. But Dawson knew the significance of late December.

"Well as could be expected," he told his friend.

"You'll call me…"

"I will. If I need to."

With that promise extracted, Dawson said his goodbyes. Still focusing on his computer, Jack told Mia, "Give me a minute," then typed in the last few notes from the meeting.

Had anyone else asked him how he was, Jack would have glad-handed them. But Dawson was the only one who'd stuck by him every moment, through Jack's arrest and the trial. He'd been the one to sit with Jack as he got quietly drunk that first anniversary. Dawson been the only one to believe in him.

Except for Joanna Sanchez, or rather, the woman Joanna pretended to be. For those few short weeks before Dawson uncovered Joanna's duplicity, Jack had clung to her, desperate for her kindness, her promise of love. If not for Dawson, who'd outted the woman after seeing her byline and photo on the Web, Jack would have spilled his guts to her, and consequently seen every detail of his life with Elizabeth exposed in the press.

Which only made it all the more imperative that he keep straight in his head who Mia was. She seemed nice, she seemed kind. She might not have an agenda like Joanna did, but if and when she figured out who he was, her attitude toward him would change. Like everyone else in his life—Dawson excepted—she wouldn't be able to put aside that suspicion.

He finally turned to her. She was gazing out the window, a look of pure enchantment on her face. "The sun is out."

He pushed his chair around to get a better view. The pristine snow sparkled, icy jewels scattered across its surface by a generous hand. Even though he'd seen this view before, had soaked in its beauty, seeing the joy reflected in her soft gray eyes turned wonderment to miracle.

She smiled at him. "It would be a shame to go out there and sully all that gorgeous white. But it's so tempting. I still haven't made a snow angel."

He wanted to play like a child with her, have a snowball fight, make a fort, a snowman. All the things he and Elizabeth had talked about doing when they first bought the property. He could do them all with Mia.

He shook his head to dispel the notion. "What did you want?"

"I'd like to research memory loss. Do some searches on amnesia. Could I get some time on your computer?"

"I have a hell of a lot of proprietary information on my hard drive." Although it was all password protected. He could set up a separate account for her that wouldn't have access to his sensitive data.

Her gaze fixed on a black computer bag beside his desk. "Is there a laptop in there?"

He'd forgotten about his old notebook computer. "It's ancient. The processor's slow."

"I don't mind." She tipped her chin up in challenge.

He groped for further justification to dissuade her from using the laptop. "The wireless card went out and I never replaced it."

"I wouldn't be able to get online?"

He considered telling her no, she wouldn't. But the lie didn't sit right. "I could set you up with a CAT-5 cable. But you'd only be able to access the Internet here in my office."

Which meant she'd be surfing the Web only a few feet from him. If it had been difficult keeping his mind focused on work with Mia in the next room, how would he manage it with her beside him?

He had to move several towering stacks of paper from a side table to make room for the laptop. Once he got the power cord and the blue cable plugged into the back of the laptop, he pressed the on button. "Haven't used it in months. Might not even boot."

But the computer completed the boot sequence flawlessly. An icon in the system tray told him the Internet connection was functional. Jack retreated to his own chair, wishing he had the materials to build a wall partitioning his office.

He couldn't keep his gaze from straying toward her. She operated the computer with ease, double-clicking the browser and rapidly typing search terms into his favorite search engine.

"There's another entry on the list of things you're good at," Jack said, watching her.

"Computers. Cooking. Drawing. Science." She ticked the items off on her fingers. "But what does it all mean? It's not as if I could enter those into a search box and Mia would pop up, complete with my full identity."

"They're obviously a significant part of you," he pointed out. "You do them without thinking, without having to work at it."

"But it still gets me nowhere." She stabbed the touchpad on the laptop, bringing up a new screen. "Maybe one of these Web sites will give me some answers."

Over her shoulder, he read the home-page title. "Psychogenic amnesia." She leaned into the screen as she read, as if to better extract from the text the secrets her mind had hidden. Her hands lay on the keyboard, tension in the set of her fingers.

He wanted to reach across, take her hand. Assure her she'd find herself again. Soothe that furrow between her eyes, the tightness in her shoulders.

Here was the real danger in sharing this space with her. He was so raw, so torn open, he couldn't keep his emotions straight. Just as he'd raced headlong into a relationship with the scheming Joanna, he was at risk of convincing himself that holding Mia in his arms would heal him.

Turning away from her, he opened the several documents and spreadsheets that next needed his attention. He'd learned over the years to compartmentalize himself; he would have gone mad otherwise. Now he used that knack to close himself off, building a mental box around himself. He strengthened its walls and seams until he felt quite alone, until he could almost believe that Mia was no longer there.

He couldn't hold back the despair. But he told himself that didn't matter.

While Jack's voice rumbled in her ear, Mia clicked through to one Web site after another that dealt with psychogenic and dissociative amnesia, searching for some kind of holy grail to shed light on her blocked memories. Some of the pieces targeted the layperson, others were geared toward professionals, the sophistication of the terminology varying with the audience. The more technical the language, the more comfortable she felt reading it—she could separate herself from the condition, pretend her research was for someone beside herself.

"Dissociative amnesia." She read the frightening diagnosis with as much dispassion as she could muster. "Inability to remember past experiences or personal information." She fit that to a T.

"Usually caused by a stressful or traumatic event." But what? A car accident, Jack had suggested. But when she pictured in her mind driving, losing control of the vehicle, careening off the road, she didn't feel any particular distress. Nothing like the black fear that visited her in her nightmares, had attacked her that day in the snow.

She scanned the list of treatments. Psychotherapy, cognitive therapy, hypnosis. Art therapy. She glanced over at Jack, saw the headset still in place. He listened intently to whatever the caller was saying, then with mouse clicks interspersed, typed at his keyboard.

As he turned to grab a file, he caught her looking at him. The manila folder he'd just laid his fingers on slithered to the floor, the papers scattering. She saw irritation in his face and something darker, meaner, in his eyes. Fear bubbled up inside her.

"I'm sorry," she said softly.

"Dammit, I have to call you back," he barked into the headset. He tore the device from his head and threw it toward his desk. It bounced off the monitor and to the floor.

When he turned back toward her, the breath caught in her throat. His dark eyes now blazed with anger, turned blue-black in their rage. As she watched, his hair, sleek and straight, seemed to change shape, grow shorter, curlier, paler in color.

She tried to shake off the hallucination, to see the real man beneath it. Told herself, *This is Jack. He won't hurt you. There's no reason to be afraid.* She forced herself to kneel on the floor to help gather up the mess. But she kept one eye on him, on the face that wasn't Jack's face.

Then his hand brushed against her left arm, and pain lanced through her. She gasped, scrambling away from him.

He sat back on his heels. "What's wrong?"

For a moment, the healing scratch on her left arm turned bloody again, the wound throbbing with pain. Then her vision cleared and the phantom blood vanished. Jack's face resolved into its familiar features, his dark eyes concerned.

She levered herself back up in her chair, edged it backward. Felt close to tears. "I thought you were going to hit me."

He stared at her as if she'd grown a second head. "Why in God's name would I do that?"

"I don't know." She tried to swallow past a tight throat. "You looked so angry. Your face…"

He kept his gaze fixed on her as he finished gathering the papers. "I'm going to call Dawson back, tell him we'll have to continue the meeting later. Then we'll get some lunch."

She nodded, swiping away the tear that had escaped down her cheek. Too unsettled to continue her research, she shut the laptop, then left Jack's office. She sat cross-legged on the floor in front of the fire, shivering despite its cheerful glow.

A few minutes later, Jack put out a hand to help her up. "Sit in the kitchen with me while I heat some soup."

She hesitated before laying her hand in his. Shaking off the renewed spurt of fear, she let him pull her to her feet. He let go immediately, and she followed him to the kitchen.

While she seated herself at the breakfast bar, he opened two cans of soup. "What happened?"

She dragged in a calming breath. "When the papers fell and you were so angry—"

About to pour the soup into a saucepan, he looked over at her. "I wasn't angry. Annoyed at my clumsiness maybe, but not mad."

"I saw something…different in your face." Rubbing at her brow, she tried to remember. Realization struck her like a burst of light. "I was seeing someone else. Someone who was angry. Enraged," she finished on a bare whisper.

"Who?" Jack asked.

Her stomach clenching at the memory, she forced herself to remember. "Blue eyes. Short, curly blond hair. Maybe… smaller than you."

"Any idea who he is?"

Pursuing the memory, she felt like a magnet, her north pole facing the north pole of the mystery man. They repelled each other, an invisible force rejecting both bodies.

Then a curtain dropped, obscuring the face. She huffed with impatience. "It's gone."

He stirred the soup as it heated. "Have you learned anything on the Web this morning?"

Too restless to sit, she busied herself slicing bread and arranging it on a plate. "With simple amnesia, physical damage leads to a loss of information. But assuming what I'm experiencing is dissociative amnesia, my memories still exist, but they're deeply buried. By some theoretical traumatic event."

"Which you also can't remember."

His tone was neutral, but frustration welled up in her anyway. "Of course I can't! It's part of the whole process. If I blocked anything, it would be the event itself."

He served up soup and they sat opposite each other at the breakfast bar. "And if you could remember that trauma…"

She couldn't suppress a shudder. "The rest of it would probably come back."

Even considering the possibility closed her throat, set off a tremor in her hand as she took a sip of the beef barley soup. Crawling down that tunnel of fire just to confront the monster at the end was unthinkable. She'd rather crawl into a hole somewhere, pretend her past never existed.

But as much as she might wish it, she couldn't just start her life over from this point. She couldn't keep her past buried because she was too much of a coward to face it.

Her appetite for the soup gone, she forced herself to eat several spoonfuls then picked up the slice of sourdough bread. Agitated, she twisted the crust off to give her hands something to do. "You said your wife was a psychologist?"

Sopping up the last of his soup with his bread, he eyed her warily. "Yes."

"Is there anything…" Her throat bone dry, she took a sip of water. "Are there any methods she might have talked about that could work for me?"

He stared at her, mouth open. She could see him consider an option, then just as quickly reject it. "No."

"What were you thinking just now?"

"I'm not a psychotherapist, Mia. I'm the last person who should be mucking around in your head." He went to the sink, back to her as he rinsed his bowl.

She moved up beside him with her own dishes. "But if you know something that could help—"

"It's nothing." He shook her uneaten lunch down the garbage disposal. "A relaxation technique. It crossed my mind it might work for you, to get past the fear. But I don't know what I'm doing, Mia. I could make things worse."

She grabbed his arm, turning him around toward her. "What if I want to risk it? Shouldn't that be my choice?"

"Except if you got hurt, that would be on my head." Under her hand, his arm flexed, the muscles as hard as stone. If she stroked him there, would that tension ease? If she put her arms around him, would he hold her as he had last night?

She stepped out of reach. "Still, I'd like to try it."

He shut off the water, dried his hands. "It's a damn bad idea."

"Please, Jack. I'm getting nowhere trying to remember on my own."

His gaze fixed on her for a long moment, then he nodded in reluctant assent. "After dinner."

She should have just said thank you and walked out of the room. Instead, gripped by impulse, she rose up on tiptoe and pressed her mouth to his. A quick kiss to express her gratitude transformed into light and heat in a flashover moment.

He pulled her against him, one hand at the small of her back, the other at the nape of her neck. Excitement shot up her spine at the feel of him, hard against her belly, the curl of his hot breath against her face. She felt consumed by him, incinerated by the flame of their sudden passion.

She would have done anything in that moment—let him strip her naked, take her on the cool tile of the kitchen floor. Anything that would blot out the doubt, the questions, the myriad unknowns.

With a gasp she pulled back from him, jamming herself up against the counter. His chest heaved, his dark eyes looked dazed. He lifted one hand as if to reach for her again, then strode from the kitchen as if pursued by demons.

She felt pretty crazed herself. Raising a trembling hand to her mouth, still feeling the pressure of Jack's kiss, she retreated to her room. As she sank onto the bed, her hand fell on the art pad. Leaning against the pillows, she propped her legs up to act as an easel, and picked up the pencil.

She shut her eyes, let herself drift. She tried to picture the face she'd seen overlaid on Jack's, the angry eyes, the rage-twisted mouth. Instead of sketching only what was in front of her, maybe she could draw that face from that memory.

At the edge of her awareness, she heard Jack slam shut the door to his office. Despite what had happened in the kitchen, knowing he was nearby gave her a sense of security. She opened her eyes, let her hand move. The pencil seemed to lay lines on the paper of its own accord.

Head down, she kept her focus, ignoring the cramp in her hand, the stiffness in her neck. She didn't know how long she drew, but by the time her hand finally stilled and she looked up, the shadows of the trees had lengthened across the snow outside. Late afternoon, which meant she'd been drawing nearly two hours.

Setting down the pencil, she let her gaze fall on the sketch in her lap. Her heart fell when she saw what she had drawn in such careful detail. Not a window into her past, but a view of the present.

Unsmiling, but his eyes soft and kind, a near perfect depiction of Jack Traynor stared up at her from the page.

The last of the dinner dishes stowed in the dishwasher, Jack pressed the start button and dried his hands on a kitchen towel. Mia waited for him in the great room, her game smile as she'd left the kitchen not quite masking the apprehension in her eyes. The savory meal she'd prepared—beef stew and biscuits—sat like a rock in his stomach. His dread of making a mistake with Mia competed with the increasing pain of the impending anniversary.

Stuffing the towel over the handle of the oven door, he strode into the great room. Seeing Mia there on the sofa, huddled and small, all his misgivings exploded. What the hell did he think he was doing? He wasn't Elizabeth, with a doctoral degree in clinical psychology and thousands of hours of counseling experience. What he knew about Mia's condition he could fit into a micrometer.

"Ready to delve into my darkest thoughts?" Her voice trembled, her smile faltering.

"This might not do a damn thing for you." He switched off the room lights, leaving just the fire for illumination. "Probably won't."

She let out a long gust of air. "Maybe."

Elizabeth had taught him the relaxation technique during

grad school, when the stress of finishing his doctoral thesis had overwhelmed him. Everything had come at him too fast— starting at UC Berkeley at age sixteen, earning his BA in three years and launching into the doctoral program in civil engineering. By the time he started work on his thesis at twenty-three, he was on the brink of burnout. Then he met Elizabeth, two years older and much more grounded. She'd saved his life.

If only he could have returned the favor five years ago.

He focused back on Mia. "Lie down."

She'd stacked two pillows from the bedroom against the arm of the sofa and now she leaned against them. She shut her eyes, her fingers laced together, the tension in them clear.

He sat at the end of the sofa. Her feet, in a pair of Elizabeth's white ankle socks, were just shy of his legs. He remembered sitting like this with his wife, rubbing her feet, a prelude sometimes to lovemaking.

Except this wasn't Elizabeth and he damn well wasn't going to think about sex. "Let go of your hands, let them fall to your sides," he told Mia.

Once her hands lay slack, he started on the script he remembered Elizabeth using. "Starting with your feet, relax the tension. Imagine the tightness as rosebuds. As they bloom, the petals relax, one layer after another. Each breath relaxes them even more."

That had been Elizabeth's imagery; he felt awkward using her words. But he could see the tautness ease, Mia's toes uncurl, feet dropping to either side in relaxation.

"After your feet, move up to your ankles…" He could imagine his hand there at her ankle. "…calves…" Fingers stroking upward. "…knees…" Dipping into that indentation where her leg folded. "…thighs…" Palm cupping the tender skin just before the apex.

His voice had grown raw, hoarse, as blood beat hard and hot low in his body. He yanked himself out of his fantasies, shutting his eyes to Mia lying there. He would have moved from the sofa to the recliner, but he would risk disturbing Mia from the calm the exercise had instilled in her.

He had to do a little of his own creative imagery, picturing his body a million miles away, only his voice lingering here in the dim, fire-lit room. His words took on an hypnotic rhythm, and he realized his own tension had seeped away. At the same time, a chord of awareness, a bright white connection had formed between him and Mia.

He'd felt this with Elizabeth. The scientist in him would reject it as a trick of the mind, an illusion. But he couldn't deny the way it steadied him, filled him with peace. Each breath he would take during those sessions with Elizabeth would move from her, through him and back through her again.

As it did now with Mia. He didn't have to open his eyes to see that her chest rose and fell in perfect timing with his own. Didn't have to feel her pulse to know it beat in tandem with his.

In this crystalline moment, they'd become one being. This was far more intimate than lovemaking and far more dangerous.

He pushed himself to continue, moving to the next step in Elizabeth's process. "In this moment you are protected. No matter what your mind remembers, you are perfectly safe."

What now? Where did he take her? Certainly not into the moment of the trauma, but how far back? Again he felt the weight of his ineptitude. He could so easily mess this up.

"Inside your bubble of safety, go back to a month ago," he said softly. "It's an ordinary day. You wake up in bed. Turn to look beside you." He forced out the next question. "Is there someone there with you?"

Her breathing lost its steady rhythm. Her fingers flexed at her sides, her legs shifted. Tension seemed to crawl back up her body.

He had to pull her out of wherever he'd put her, and quickly. "You've left your house, still safe, still protected. You're at work now."

He waited until she relaxed again, the momentary distress draining away. "Where are you? What do you see?"

She answered in a near whisper. "I'm at a desk. A well-lit room. Lots of other people."

"Do you recognize any of them? Are they coworkers?"

"No. They're people I work with but not…" She reached out, as if to grasp the truth. "It's a classroom. They're my students."

"You're a teacher."

"There's a periodic table of the elements on the wall. A model of DNA." Her brilliant smile took his breath away. "I'm a science teacher."

"Can you see your name anywhere? Hear anyone calling it?"

"Yes. Someone new just entered. He's coming to the front of the room…"

"Do you see his face—"

"No!" Bolt upright, eyes still closed, she clutched Jack's arm. "Don't— No!"

"Mia! You're safe. Open your eyes. You're here with me. You're safe."

Her eyes snapped open, clouded with whatever horror she'd seen in her mind. Then she threw her arms around him and he pulled her into his lap. She shuddered so hard, he was terrified he'd sent her over the edge, into some dark land she'd never be able to return from. He could only murmur soft comfort, stroke her back, press his mouth against her hair.

The spell they'd woven had broken. Her breathing was erratic and where his fingers rested on her neck, her heart beat in a crazy syncopation. His face buried in her hair, he wished he could breathe calm back into her, could erase whatever had frightened her so.

"We should talk about it," he whispered.

She shook her head against his chest.

"While it's still fresh in your mind—"

"I don't want to think about it." She tipped her head back. "Tell me something about your life. Something happy. So I don't have to remember."

He wanted to argue with her, tell her there had been damn little happiness in his life. A father who walked out, renouncing his own family in favor of a new wife and her young children. A mother, hit hard by her husband's abandonment, who couldn't grasp her son's brilliant mind and left the nurturing to her older daughter. Then Jack's own wife, the love of his life, murdered.

But Mia implored him with her eyes, and he couldn't refuse. He thought back, groping for a bright moment amongst the grief.

"Elizabeth's and my first date." God, how long had it been since he'd thought about that? "What a disaster."

Mia narrowed her gaze at him. "This is a *happy* memory?"

He couldn't suppress a smile as he remembered. "Blew a tire on the way to the restaurant and had no idea how to fix it. It was Elizabeth who found the jack and tire iron and got it changed."

She'd hiked up her skirt to get it out of the way and he'd

ogled her legs the entire time. "We were so late we lost our reservation. Had to wait an hour to be seated. Then after dinner, I realized I'd left my wallet at home."

"So Elizabeth had to pay," Mia said.

"I was twenty-three years old and she was twenty-five. I'd desperately wanted to impress her. By the time I drove her home, I was sure I'd lost any chance of ever seeing her again."

"So, what happened?"

He hesitated, the details of those moments on Elizabeth's doorstep as clear in his mind as if it had only been last week and not thirteen years ago. Her kiss had curled his toes, all but stopped his heart.

"Let's just say," Jack said, tucking the memories away again deep inside, "we came to an amicable agreement."

Sighing, Mia smiled. "I wish I could have met her."

He could so easily see Elizabeth and Mia laughing together, sharing their joy in a way special to women. The injustice of Elizabeth's death rolled over him with a wave of pain.

Holding Mia only thrust the knife deeper into his chest. He couldn't have Elizabeth back and he didn't dare let Mia in. He couldn't depend on her comfort, not when she'd be out of his life so soon.

He eased away from her, the knot of pain tightening inside him. He groped in his mind for an excuse to leave. "There's something I forgot I have to get done tonight. If you're okay…"

Her eyes glittered in the firelight as she gazed up at him. "I'm fine."

She didn't sound it, but he wasn't in any state of mind to dig deeper. He backed away, then headed for his office.

Once he got inside and shut the door, he didn't even turn

Christmas without him had been harder than she'd expected, and she was in tears after decorating the apartment alone.

He couldn't remember the words he'd flung at her, her biting response. It wasn't like them to argue, and it caught them both off guard. Their mutual apology before they'd said goodbye had been three parts exhaustion and one part remorse.

Jack had vowed to make it up to her when he returned home Christmas Eve. He'd left Dawson in the lurch the next morning, arriving an hour late for Saturday's conference presentation, spending the time shopping for the perfect necklace for Elizabeth.

A necklace he never gave her. He was carrying it in his pocket the day they arrested him for her murder. When he was released on bail and had his property returned to him, he had Dawson stop at a local thrift store so he could donate the pricy piece of jewelry. Weighted with regrets, it was far to heavy to carry around anymore.

He dragged his sorry self out of bed and into the bathroom. A hot shower left him clean without washing away the sense of dread that haunted him. He wasn't looking forward to seeing Mia, the what-ifs she represented just as painful as the might-have-beens of his short marriage.

As he strode through the great room toward the kitchen, he spotted her in the living-room window seat, a paperback in her lap, her gaze directed out at the snowy day. She wore one of Elizabeth's flannel shirts, red and blue plaid over a blue turtleneck, her feet in thick red socks. As he passed her, she glanced at him, nodding a silent hello before returning her attention to the icy winter panorama outside.

Resisting the temptation to sit beside her, he kept himself moving toward the kitchen. A still-warm loaf of some kind of fragrant spice bread with a few slices gone sat on the counter on a wooden cutting board. A mixing bowl and baking pan air-dried in the dish drainer.

He cut himself two thick pieces of bread, then poured a mug of coffee, consuming both while standing at the breakfast bar. As he ate, his gaze locked on Mia and he felt a hunger he knew wouldn't be satisfied by the sweet spice bread.

Serving himself a second cup of coffee, he padded out to the great room and sat on the hope chest. "Did you sleep okay?"

"Sure." But when she turned toward him, he could see the circles under her eyes. "I've torn through so many of Elizabeth's books, I can't stand the thought of reading another page. I even cleaned the bathroom and kitchen this morning just for a little variety."

"You didn't have to do that."

She shrugged. "Is there anything else I could do for you?"

The leading question dangled there between them for several seconds. There was a whole list of things she could do for him he had no intention of identifying.

His mind lit on what seemed like a safe enough option. "You could file some of the papers in my office. Most of it would be pretty easy to categorize. They need to go into file boxes for storage in the garage."

She slid from the window seat. "Lead me to it."

In his office he gestured at the piles he'd moved yesterday to give her a workspace. "There's correspondence mixed in with old contracts, brochures and plain old junk mail. Some miscellaneous odds and ends." Pulling out samples of each type of item he needed sorted, he laid them out on the floor. "Just put them in piles, then order them by date if they've got one. I'll find you the file boxes."

While she got started, Jack scouted out the plastic boxes he had stacked in the garage. Of the three he found, only one was empty; the others were packed full. Back in his office, he scrounged up some hanging folders and handed them and the file box to Mia.

Focusing on his computer, he did what he could to block her out. But with the approaching holiday, all of his clients had shut down their operations early. The meetings that usually filled his Fridays had been canceled. Even Dawson planned to leave by three and had tied up all his loose ends with Jack yesterday.

Jack had nothing but a handful of miscellaneous housekeeping tasks he'd put off for when he had the time. Backing up files and data, digging through the dozens of nonwork-related e-mails he had tucked away in a temporary folder, answering those that required a response. Archiving folders no longer in current use. Dull drudgery that wasn't nearly enough distraction from Mia, who sat on the floor within arm's reach.

Of course, she couldn't do the filing work with no interaction or his guidance. She'd ask for clarification on this or that piece of paper, sometimes holding it up for him to see, sometimes bringing it over, hovering beside his chair while he examined it. She'd rolled up the cuffs of the shirt and pushed up the sleeves of the turtleneck, and as she stood there, he could see her pulse fluttering in her wrist.

At one o'clock she rose, throwing her arms over her head in a mesmerizing stretch that pulled the hem of the turtleneck from the waist of her jeans. The motion exposed a pale swath of her slender waist, her navel winking briefly into view. When she asked if he was ready for lunch, he could barely muster a coherent response.

He stayed in his office until she called him, then wolfed down the grilled ham and cheese she'd made, washing it down with milk. After lunch he was grateful the trash was full, because it gave him the excuse to go outside to dump the plastic bag into the thirty-gallon garbage can. He stood out there as long as he could stand the cold, the house eaves scant shelter from the drifting snow.

She took a break after lunch, going back to her sketch pad, returning to the filing in late afternoon. He'd gotten little accomplished during his time alone, fantasies of Mia dragging him all too willingly away from his work.

She finally had the piles sorted shortly before six. He gave up the impossible task of ignoring her, allowing himself to watch as she inserted an identifying tab into each hanging folder, then filed the stacks of paper into their appropriate slots.

She ran out of room in the plastic box with two piles yet to file. Sitting back on her heels, she asked, "Is there another file box?"

"No. Just leave those."

"There's a box in the guest-room closet." She levered herself up. "I moved it to make room for a laundry pile. It felt close to empty."

She walked out before he could stop her, her scent drifting toward him as she passed. Pressing his thumb between his brows, he tried to remember a file box in the closet. When it came back to him what he had tossed in there four months ago, he was on his feet running toward the guest room.

But she'd already opened the box when he got there. From the color in her cheeks he knew she'd moved aside the empty manila folders and unearthed what they'd hidden. A forgotten box of condoms.

She dropped the folders and let the plastic lid fall shut. "Sorry." The color flagging her cheeks deepened.

Walk away, he told himself. Don't think about what's under those folders.

Except that was all he *could* think about, that and the way Mia's lush lips would feel against his, how her mouth would taste. The moans she would make as he touched her, the way she would feel when she fell apart in his arms.

If he'd had a scrap of nobility in him, he would have turned and left the room. But then her head tipped up, her gaze meeting his as her lush lips parted. And chivalry was the last damn thing on his mind.

She unfolded herself from the floor, reaching for him. "I know we shouldn't. I don't even know who I am. But wanting you… It's the only thing about me that's real."

That was all the invitation he needed. He lowered his mouth to hers, groaned with the first hot contact. The heat burned away his misgivings, silenced the warnings his mind screamed. All that mattered was the feel of Mia in his arms.

Kissing her, sensations rocketing through him, he backed her toward the bed. He drew her down with him, the slight weight of her body on his an exquisite pleasure. Her hands on his face, her hips pressed into his, the sound of her breathing threatened to push him over the edge far too soon.

He dragged in a harsh breath, struggling for control. Twisting, he eased her around and under him. Up on his elbows, an inch of space between them, he inhaled, exhaled, tempering the heat of his body.

She waited, watching him. Smiled up at him. Then when he lowered himself against her, she sighed, eyes fluttering shut.

Slowing the pace, he brushed his mouth against hers, drawing the tip of his tongue across her lower lip. Her lips parted, inviting him in, but he resisted temptation. Instead he trailed kisses across her cheek, along her jaw to the point of her chin, back to her mouth. He painted her lower lip with his tongue again, then grazed kisses along her throat, to the shell of her ear.

She squirmed under him, and the wildland fire within him nearly jumped its containment. He took another long breath, reveling in her heady scent, regaining control.

Lifting her, he stripped the flannel shirt and tossed it aside. The turtleneck underneath was rucked up, exposing her narrow waist. The peaks of her nipples strained through the thin knit, and he realized she wasn't wearing a bra. His excitement ratcheted up another notch.

Hooking his thumbs in the hem of the turtleneck, he stroked her along her rib cage as he slowly slipped it from her. The hem caught on her nipples, and as the knit brushed against them, she gasped and threw her head back. Keeping the turtleneck where it was, he bent his head and laved her nipple, wetting the knit. Her hips lifted from the bed, pressing into his.

Easing off her turtleneck, he arched back to look at her lying half-naked beneath him. Her eyes were half-lidded with passion, her cheeks stained pink. Her chest rose and fell as she breathed, her small breasts trembling with the motion.

He lowered himself again, his hand drifting along her rib cage, thumb grazing the curve of her breast. Her breath hitched as he lingered there, as he brushed kisses along the tender skin of her throat to her collarbone. His hand continued down her body to the waistband of her jeans, around the front to the button.

He'd just unfastened it when a shred of reason intruded. His hand stilled and he whispered in her ear. "Protection."

He rose from the bed, lifting the lid on the plastic file box and pulling out the condoms inside. It crossed his mind that this moment of separation could give her a chance for second thoughts. Even as his body declared its outrage at that possibility, the one speck of his brain still clear enough to think realized it would be better for both of them if she changed her mind.

But she said nothing as he returned to the bed and set the box of condoms on the nightstand. When he leaned over her again, she twined her arms around his neck and pulled him down to kiss her. His hands splayed across her belly, he soaked in her scent, her feel, the small moans his touch brought from her throat.

She shivered, reminding him how cool the room was. Pushing aside the covers on the bed, he urged her into it. While she lay back on the pillows, he undressed, throwing aside sweater and shoes, shucking his jeans. As he shoved off his shorts, her avid gaze on him nearly stopped his heart. He was glad she still wore her jeans, that there was something to slow him down.

He knelt on the bed beside her. His hands shook so badly, he fumbled the zipper on her jeans. With gritted teeth, he slid it down, then tugged off jeans and panties. He looked his fill, from head to toe, then back up to the dark nest of curls between her legs.

He turned off the light, wanting the intimacy of the darkness. He could barely manage the condom, his fingers clumsy as he ripped open the packet then sheathed himself. "It's been a damn long time," he told her roughly. "I don't know if I can…"

Her hand on his arm, she pulled him down to her. He settled between her thighs, lost in heaven. Just lying so close to her, skin to skin, was paradise.

He reached between their bodies and slipped a finger inside her. Her wet, hot readiness set off a roaring in his ears. Holding on to a last scrap of self-control, he spread his palm against her. Her sighs intensified to moans, the sound growing more guttural as he thrust a second finger inside her. Her wetness soaked his palm, her pleasure pounding inside him.

She exploded against his hand, tightening rhythmically around his fingers. While her body still vibrated with her climax, he pushed inside her, sucking in a breath as fire lit his loins.

Wanting desperately to take his time, he knew his body had waited long enough. He thrust deep, her legs wrapping around his hips, ankles locking at the small of his back.

She reached down, her fingernails digging into his hips as she urged him closer. He bucked into her, the exquisite sensation nearly agonizing. He held back as long as he could, then climaxed with a cry of triumph, feeling her pulse around him as pleasure overwhelmed her again.

Bit by bit, he came back to himself, became aware of the sound of her breathing as it slowed, the relaxation of her body that told him she was asleep. He levered his weight off her carefully, then went into the bathroom across the hall to clean up.

When he stepped back into the bedroom, stood over the bed watching her, he tried to grasp the emotions rocketing around inside him. Regret or awkwardness he would have understood. Instead, he felt shell-shocked and vulnerable, all his secrets exposed. Their lovemaking had been too intense, had reached far too deeply inside him.

If he knew what was good for him, he would back away, go back to his office or to his own room. Try to find a way to drive Mia from his mind. Even as the sensations still scudded across his skin, he knew he shouldn't let his body record their passion.

But his body had its own agenda. Without thinking, he lay beside her again, fitting himself against her. His arm sliding under her, he pulled her against him, nestling her head just under his chin. Just for a few moments…then he would get up, start the business of shutting Mia out again. He would only close his eyes for a few moments.

Her warmth seeped into him, and he fell asleep.

It seemed only a heartbeat later that he jolted awake. Dim nightmare images lingered in his mind, talons of the past digging into his unconscious. His heart slammed in his chest, and his breathing was ragged.

Unease settling in his belly, he edged away from Mia. Her hand skimmed his chest, reaching for him even as she still slept. He longed to keep her close, to hold her against his heart. But something was crawling beneath his skin, clamoring for escape. It pushed him to his feet as his heart pounded in his ears.

His gaze fell on the clock—8:36 p.m. As his agitation grew, he remembered every detail of his argument with Elizabeth five days before her murder. The memories clung to him as if revisiting him from his nightmares.

The short, bright time with Mia in her bed had given him momentary respite from the ugliness. Like snow that eradicates everything it covers, making everything white, clean, new, Mia had lent a purity to his world.

Lent only, and now it all came crashing back. Groping in the dark, he gathered up his clothes, threw them on. He hung on to control by a thread, had to get out before it severed.

Nearly to the door, he slammed his hip into the corner of the dresser, and the wedding picture on top toppled with a clatter. Mia stirred in their bed, then buried herself deeper in the covers. He wanted so dearly to lie down with her again, to feel her heart beat against his. But he knew he had to get out.

He snatched up the photo, those happy, oblivious smiles breaking his heart. Pain like a stone in his chest drove him from the room and down the hall to his own room. Tossing the framed photo on his bed, he all but ran back down the hall to the foyer.

Fumbling for his snowboots in the coat closet, he shoved his feet into them. He wrenched his heavy parka from its hanger, scrambled for the gloves and wool hat that fell from the pockets.

He grew more frantic each moment, the clock ticking closer to 9:00 p.m., the time of his phone call with Elizabeth. In the back his mind where sanity still huddled, he knew it was foolhardy to go out with temperatures hovering in the low teens, even dressed warmly. But with his past snapping at his heels, he had no choice.

He remembered at the last moment to close the door quietly. He took off down his driveway where the drifts weren't as bad, the snow only up around his shins. Moonlight glazed the snow-burdened trees, frosting them with silver, achingly beautiful. He could only think of Elizabeth and how much she would have enjoyed the sight.

He got as far away from the house as he could before the pain erupted. It overcame him like a predator slamming him in the back, dropping him to his knees in the snow. It dug its claws in, spreading agony through him.

He screamed, rage, grief, guilt all in equal measure. He covered his face with his hands as he crouched there, ripped apart inside. He wanted to tear his heart from his chest so he wouldn't have to feel anymore.

An eternity later he dimly heard the click of a door, and he realized he hadn't gotten far enough from the house. Mia's voice, barely loud enough to hear, enfolded him.

"Jack?"

Eyes shut, icy wetness soaking into his jeans and his body spasming from the cold, he seemed to see light sifting in between his fingers. Like a talisman, Mia's face appeared in his mind's eye. He imagined her hand on his heart, soothing, protecting.

He looked back over his shoulder. He was hidden by shadows and the downward curve of the road. She stood on his porch, sheltered, but dressed only in turtleneck, jeans and sneakers. Arms wrapped around her middle, her body vibrated from the cold.

"Jack?" she called out.

He reared up from the snow, and she jumped back, startled. "Go back inside!"

"What's going on?" She started toward him, her feet enveloped by the snow. "Are you okay?"

"Go back inside!" He was too far gone to muster anything more coherent. But having her out here in the cold terrified him. He had to get her back inside where she'd be safe.

She stood her ground, stubborn despite the shudders rolling over her. "You come with me."

His heart felt as if it lay in pieces at his feet. Yet he could imagine Mia, with her clever hands, picking up the fragments, rebuilding them into something as good as new.

He didn't trust himself to speak, was afraid of what he might say. So he just closed the distance between them and turned back with her toward the house. He left his wet boots and parka by the front door, ordered her harshly to take off her wet shoes. With a rough gesture he directed her to the pellet stove.

Refilling the hopper, he set the controls to their highest level and stood as close as he could to the glowing flames. Mia shivered beside him. He could feel her gaze on him.

He wouldn't look at her, just forced out the words, "Go to bed."

"Jack—"

She laid her hand on his arm, her fingers still chilly from the outdoors. He ached to enclose her hands in his, to warm them. Pull her closer, wrap his arms around her. The hole in his chest might be impossible to heal, but maybe she could ease the agony for a night or two.

But what about when she left? He'd only be tearing open the wound again, digging the dark hole deeper. Their love-making had made everything worse, blindsiding him with hope. He couldn't let himself give in to it.

He backed away from her, turning from the fire. Tried not to think of her standing there, watching as he went to his room.

He slammed the door shut, closing himself in darkness. Then he slumped to the floor and let the pain come. Regret lodged like an arrow in his chest as he remembered the ugly words he'd flung at Elizabeth.

"I'm sorry," he whispered, "I take it back. I didn't mean it."

But his apology was five years too late.

Chapter Ten

She'd had no right to expect anything of him. She'd asked him to make love to her, not make her promises. And she'd gotten exactly what she'd asked for—glorious, brilliant moments of climax, the exultation of feeling him inside her. How could she blame him for what she was feeling now—an emotion she didn't dare name, one she was certain he wouldn't welcome.

His cry had pulled her from a deep sleep, as if the connection forged between them during those few joyful moments had alerted her to his pain. When she'd stepped outside and spotted his dark head, vivid against the snow, she'd thought he might have gone for a walk and stumbled. But the echo of his cry still rang in her ears. It might as well have been written on her heart.

He'd barely said two words to her since that night. He

hadn't commented when she'd left the box of condoms in his room on Saturday. Most of that day he'd stayed shut up in his office or his bedroom, ignoring her tap on the door telling him she'd made dinner. On Sunday, another storm came in, spilling another foot of snow. She watched it alone while Jack hid from her, either too embarrassed by what had happened, or still too wounded.

She couldn't untangle her own feelings, let alone his. Since Friday, she'd been able to draw nothing but Jack's face. Sometimes the whole face, sometimes individual features drawn in great detail—his eyes, dark with emotion, his mouth, sensual and expressive. Just the line of his jaw where it met his ear, dark straight hair tucked behind.

Even now, early Sunday evening, she sat in the window seat, drawing pad on her lap, his face gazing up at her. The sun having set long ago behind the trees, the yellow glow from the recessed lights above her illuminated the snow outside. Beyond that weak light, with the moon not yet risen, she saw only blackness between the trees. Like her mind, hiding more than it revealed.

Beside his face with its grave expression, she'd sketched Jack's open hand. She'd penciled something nestled in his palm, a jewel or a flower.

Or maybe her heart.

The sound of a door opening turned her toward his office. He didn't so much as glance her way before heading down the hall toward his room. She wanted to run after him, grab his arm and shake him. But then what? When he just stared down at her, silent and as closed off to her as those dark woods, what would she say then? How could she put into words what she wanted from him when she didn't know herself?

She eyed the open office door. Did she dare go in to use the Internet? He might ask her to leave when he returned, or do an about-face when he saw her there. Either way, she might as well get done what she could.

While she waited for the laptop to boot, she felt a prickling move up her spine. She thought it might be trepidation over Jack's reaction when he saw her there. Except it was his absence that set off the knot of apprehension in her belly. If Jack was here, he would keep her safe. But from what?

She'd just clicked on the Web browser when a voice nearly jolted her from her chair. "Hey! Dr. T.—are you there?"

The voice had come from Jack's monitor, and now she saw the boy's face displayed in a Web cam window. Seven or eight years old with cornrow braids to his shoulders and lively brown eyes, a grin lit his dark face.

Mia moved to Jack's chair, within range of the Web cam on the monitor. "Jack's in the other room. I'm Mia."

"I'm William." His brow furrowed as he studied her. "Dr. T. never has friends over. Except Dawson, and that's hardly ever. Do you like math puzzles?"

"I'm better with words. Do you like science?"

"I'm better with math. I already solved the puzzle Dr. T. gave me yesterday. I wanted him to give me another one."

She felt Jack's presence in the doorway before she turned to see him there. His gaze flicked over her, then fixed on William as he stepped inside. "Hey, buddy, what's up?"

Mia quickly surrendered the chair to him, seating herself at the laptop again. If he had a problem with her being there, he would tell her.

After she read a last few articles on dissociative amnesia, she put aside her misgivings and did a desultory search on her name linked with the bits and pieces they'd learned about her. As she paged through them, she eavesdropped on Jack's conversation with William. It didn't take long to figure out this wasn't an ordinary young boy. Jack was offering up calculus and linear algebra problems for William to solve and the boy was over the moon with excitement.

Even more surprising was Jack's interaction with William. He joked with the boy, teased him, *laughed.* The darkness that had laid so heavily on Jack the past two days seemed in temporary abeyance.

They spoke for nearly an hour, Mia listening in, more interested in William's ebullience than in the dry psychological treatises she'd been reading. She remembered Jack's guess that she was a teacher; it made sense that she felt so comfortable around a bright young boy.

"Can I say good-night to Mia, Dr. T.?"

Jack looked over his shoulder at her, his face impassive. She rolled her chair over; he backed his away.

"It was good to meet you, William," Mia said, aware of Jack sitting only inches away.

"You, too." He scrunched his face at her. "You look kind of familiar."

His simple pronouncement knocked the air from her lungs. Jack leaned into range of the Web cam. "Where do you know her from, William?"

A voice in the background shouted William's name and he turned away from the Web cam. "Just a minute, Mama!" He turned back to Jack. "I'm not sure, Dr. T. But I know I've seen her face before."

Another shout, closer now. William tossed out a hasty goodbye and broke the Web-cam connection.

Mia stared at the blank screen with frustration. "Could he have seen a missing-person report about me?"

"Hard to say. He's beyond genius—his IQ is off the charts. But he's eight years old—one minute he's solving game theory problems, the next he's forgetting to take out the trash."

"He calls you Dr. T."

Something in his expression told her she'd sidled into dangerous territory. But he answered her question. "I was a professor of civil engineering before I started my business."

He pushed back in his chair, looking past her out the window. The snowfall had thinned, a few flakes scattering in the breeze past the window.

They couldn't ignore forever what had happened on Friday. But she was so grateful to have him talking to her again, she stuck to safer topics. "How did you meet William?"

"Dawson met his mother back in April when he was on a business trip in Chicago."

A ray of sunlight punched through the clouds, brightening the room. She felt a sudden urgency to capture the look of that light on Jack's face, the way it softened his eyes. An even stronger temptation arose in her to trace the line of his jaw, his mouth, with her fingers.

She clenched her hands in her lap. "Is she a client of yours?"

The sunlight faded and shadows fell on Jack's face again. "She was on the cleaning crew in the client's building. Dawson struck up a conversation with her. She told him all about William, how proud she was of him."

"You mentor him, then."

"I remember how it was, always being the smartest kid in the room. And in my case and William's, the smallest."

She couldn't help it; she scanned his six-foot-plus body

head to toe. His mouth curved into a smile, not as broad as the one he'd given William, but genuine. "I was a late bloomer."

"I've known kids like him." She blinked in surprise. "Not sure where that came from. But I can see their faces."

His fingers interlaced across his lean belly. "Can we talk about the relaxation exercise?"

Her stomach lurched. From his determined expression, she could see there was no avoiding the discussion this time.

"When I had you wake in bed, look to see if someone was there with you…"

Now a kernel of fear stabbed her. "Yes."

"You were afraid." His gaze met hers. "What did you see?"

She groped for his hand without thinking, his warm palm against hers giving her courage. "There was a man there with me."

"Your husband?"

The significance of the question hung in the air. If she was married, what they'd done Friday night… "I don't think so." She tested the notion inside herself, looked for honesty rather than self-serving expedience. Found surety there. "No, not my husband. I'm not married."

"A boyfriend?"

A rock fell in her stomach, a boulder. "No," she whispered.

"What was he doing in bed with you?"

She shook her head. "Maybe what I was seeing isn't what really happened. Maybe my imagination put him there."

His gaze narrowed on her. "But why?"

"I don't know! I only know…"

"He terrified you."

Even now, remembering, she found it hard to breathe. She nodded.

"And then, at work," Jack continued. "You were happy at first. You saw your students, your classroom. But then—"

The tendons popped out on her hands as she gripped Jack's. "He came in."

"The same man."

"I think so." She shut her eyes, tried to recall what she'd seen. "Curly blond hair. But it's a blank where his face should be."

Her teeth chattered, despite the warmth of the room. Her heart pounded in her ears and it seemed the walls were moving closer.

"That's enough." Jack pulled her from the chair. "Let's get dinner started."

She felt nauseous at the thought of eating, but she knew he was right—she had to go do something, get busy. She'd remembered more when she wasn't trying than she did when it was her sole focus.

They threw together a quick pantry meal, combining canned clams and anchovies, lemon, garlic and olive oil with pasta to make linguini with white clam sauce. Jack found sourdough rolls in the freezer for garlic bread, and they used a last bag of lettuce for a salad.

The aroma of sautéed garlic and anchovies renewed her appetite. But as they seated themselves at the dining-room table, Mia knew they weren't finished. Jack might want to avoid the subject, but she intended to bring it front and center.

"There was more to Friday night," she said as she twirled linguini on her fork.

He glanced over at her before fixing his gaze back on his plate. "What do you want me to say, Mia? We made love. It was consensual. And best I can tell, we both enjoyed it."

His cut-and-dried assessment didn't surprise her. What

she thought she'd seen in his dark gaze did. A moment of vulnerability.

But she had to have imagined it. Wishful thinking. "If you're afraid I expect anything of you, I don't." That tasted like a lie on her tongue.

"Good." He didn't look at her this time.

They finished their meal in silence, the air all but crackling with tension. With one last bombshell hovering over the table, unasked questions rolled through Mia's mind.

Jack finally pushed his plate away, the gesture slow, deliberate. He stared down at his hands, flexing and relaxing his fingers. Then he lifted his gaze to Mia.

"She died five years ago, Christmas Eve."

Mia took a sip from her water glass, waited for him to continue. He let out a breath, heaviness in the sound.

"The week leading up to that night is…difficult." He leaned his arms on the table. "For the past four years I've made sure to spend that time alone. For privacy. This is the first year…"

"Someone's been with you."

"What you saw Friday night…" His hands tightened into fists on the table. "That's not the worst of it. That was only the prelude."

She wanted to rub his shoulder, put her arms around him. But he was so taut, she was afraid if she touched him, he'd explode. "I can't imagine how hard it must be to lose someone you love so dearly."

"If it was just grief…" He laughed, a hollow sound. "You want desperately to retrieve your memories. I would give anything to forget. To wipe away everything from that night."

He said the last savagely, shoving to his feet. Grabbing their dishes, he stacked them together with a clatter. He all but threw them into the sink, and she could hear one shatter against the stainless basin.

Hands propped on the counter, he considered the mess he'd made in the sink. "Just to be clear—what happened between us Friday night shouldn't have. It's all I can do to hold myself together."

Reaching for the broken plate, he dumped the shards into the trash. Mia felt as if he'd discarded those moments in bed together along with them.

"I'm sorry." Her throat ached, tears burning at her eyes. I shouldn't have—"

"It has nothing to do with you." His head swung toward her as a tear spilled down her cheek. "Dammit," he muttered, then pulled her into his arms. He held her against his warm, strong body, an anchor against the whirlwind.

"Don't ask me for anything else, Mia," he murmured into her hair.

Later they sat together in the great room, Jack in the recliner pretending to read a magazine, Mia curled up on the sofa with her sketch pad. She'd found a bag of some fancy cinnamon tea in the cupboard, something Dawson must have brought on one of his visits. She'd brewed enough for both of them and had finished hers; his cup had grown cold on the end table beside him.

Watching her, he knew he was only fooling himself if he thought he could touch her, comfort her, without wanting far more than that. As fractured as he was becoming as the days unwound to Christmas Eve, he still wanted Mia back in his bed, her naked body against his. Even now, it took everything in him to keep from carrying her off into the bedroom.

Of the few women he'd slept with in the years since Elizabeth's death, none of them came close to matching what he'd felt with his late wife. Joanna Sanchez, for all her professions of undying love, had been cold and distant in bed, the sex act no doubt just part of the job for her. Thankfully, she'd left the details of their intimacy out of the articles she wrote about him.

But Mia…he could still feel her body closing around his, could still hear her cries as she climaxed. Different than Elizabeth, more intensity, less abandon. But even as his emotions disintegrated inside him, his mind kept returning, again and again, to Mia's slender body in his arms.

Only because he longed for Elizabeth, because the anniversary loomed, a monstrous caricature of a Christmas gift waiting for him. Any other time of the year he could have disciplined himself, sublimated sexual desire with work. He'd done it for five years, the times he'd given in to passion a calculated effort to satisfy needs past the boiling point.

She sighed, leaning back to study what she'd drawn. She sat facing him—troubling because he could see every emotion on her face in the firelight—the pad hidden on her lap. After those first few sketches of trees and landscape, she hadn't shared her artwork. He hadn't asked, leaving it to her to offer, though he didn't like her evasiveness.

If he had chosen to take a woman to bed, to release that physical tension, it shouldn't have been someone like Mia. Even without knowing her true identity, he knew that for her it wasn't just sex. She would want commitment, the kind of forever-after he'd given up believing in.

He fixed his gaze on the fire's orange glow. Sunday night. The twenty-first of December. Five years ago today, he'd left the conference in Seattle and driven to Redmond to visit his sister and celebrate Christmas early. After his father deserted the family, his sister, Heather, a decade older than Jack, had all but raised him. After their mother died, he and Heather had lost touch, and spending those few days with her had been his way of mending fences.

He'd called Elizabeth when he'd arrived at Heather's, and the wounds they'd inflicted on each other two days before had healed. He'd still felt a guilt his apologies couldn't seem to mend. Elizabeth had seemed anxious about something, and he still hated himself for not pushing the issue.

Mia's gasp brought his attention back to her. He saw the light of realization in her face. "He's the one from my nightmares."

"Someone you drew?" He rose to take a look.

She slapped the pad shut. "No. The one I saw during the relaxation exercise."

He sat opposite her on the sofa. "He's not your husband, not a boyfriend. Could he have been a stalker?"

Hand spread, she moved it across the cover of the art pad as if contemplating what she'd drawn. "I suppose. It would explain him turning up at my classroom. He could have broken into my house."

The blood chilled in Jack's veins. "Is that what happened?"

"I have no idea." Exasperation was clear in her tone. "I'm only guessing."

She dropped the art pad on the coffee table, stretched out her legs. She wore yet another pair of Elizabeth's socks, these a whimsical lime green dotted with penguins. Elizabeth had never worn them. He'd bought them for her not long before she died.

"I'm a science teacher somewhere it doesn't snow," she said. "At a middle school—the kids looked too young to be in high school. I have a talent for sketching and crossword puzzles. I'm single."

"And your name is Mia."

"Is it?" she asked, as she had a week ago.

"Why else would you be wearing that bracelet?"

"When I saw myself in a classroom, I knew that was right. Knew I was a teacher. I'm so comfortable with the science and art—a pencil feels natural in my hand. But Mia…" She wove her fingers together. "It still doesn't feel like my name."

It startled him. He'd thought she'd accepted the name, that he'd helped her excavate at least that small part of her identity. And if indeed she wasn't Mia, if they didn't even have a name for her, how would they discover who she was?

What if they didn't? What if she truly had nowhere else to go, no other life to return to?

He squelched the joy inside him before it could so much as gain a toehold. That was the wrong damn direction to al-low his thoughts to go. Mia's future had nothing to do with him.

"Have you heard anything new about the road?" she asked.

"They're making progress, but the snow slowed every-thing down. Dawson said he might be able to get a crew up here from Arizona."

Her eyes widened. "Arizona. I've been there."

"Is that where you're from?"

He could see her struggle to retrieve the memory, her hands reaching out as if to grab it. Then she flung herself back against the arm of the sofa, her lost expression wrenching his heart. "I don't know."

He should have left it at that. Tell her she should get some sleep, that with some rest she might be able to think clearer.

But he couldn't muster the words to send her away. He wanted to lie beside her, gather her up, feel her breath against his cheek.

He had enough sense to resist that temptation. Instead he slid toward her on the sofa, settled her feet into his lap. Massaged her arches, the balls of her feet, her toes. Listened to her sighs of pleasure as he had Elizabeth's.

And he smiled, a tentative happiness welling up inside him. A fragile, delicate thing he knew he couldn't count on, wouldn't last. But for the moment he let himself enjoy it.

Chapter Eleven

Monday and Tuesday, Jack didn't hide from Mia as he had over the weekend. He'd share meals with her, sit with her in the evenings while she sketched or read. But she could sense the tension in him mounting hour by hour as Christmas Eve grew closer.

Knowing what he faced with the anniversary of his wife's death, reluctant to put her troubles on his shoulders, she kept to herself that her nightmares had returned. Her terror of falling asleep kept her reading in bed Monday and Tuesday nights until one and two in the morning, afraid to pick up the sketch pad, fearful of what her hand might draw.

Seven-thirty Wednesday morning, her eyes gritty from lack of sleep, she dragged herself from bed and stumbled into the bathroom, a change of clothes bundled in her arms. As she twisted on the shower spray, she spied the crumbs of soap in the dish and remembered she'd meant to ask Jack for another bar. She checked underneath the sink, then opened three vanity drawers before she finally spotted a familiar wrapper.

As she reached for the soap, she saw the gleam of gold. The ankle bracelet. She'd set it in here that first night before she took her shower. Had forgotten to put it back on afterward.

Setting the soap beside the sink, she picked up the bracelet, held it up to the light. Read the name worked in delicate gold. *Mia.*

Dimly she heard the rush of water from the other room, felt the air thicken with steam. Stared as the bracelet jiggled and swayed in her fingers as her hand shook. Felt the fear crawling up her spine as if it had escaped her nightmares and crept under the door after her.

As if burned, her hand jolted, and the bracelet dropped into the sink. It didn't fall down the drain as she'd feared when she first took it off, but a part of her wished it would just slither out of sight. Because she wasn't ever putting that bracelet on again. And she didn't even know why.

She threw it into the back of the drawer, slammed the drawer shut. Forgot the bar of soap and had to walk back, dripping, to get it. Stayed in the shower far longer than she should have, driven by the need to wash away whatever had clung to her fingers when she'd touched the bracelet.

When she emerged from the bathroom, dressed and finally feeling clean, there was still no sign of Jack. She started a pot of coffee, sprinkling cinnamon over the grounds, although she couldn't remember where she'd learned that trick. Then, too edgy to sit and read, she went into Jack's office and powered up the laptop.

He'd left his computer on, and when she jostled the mouse

reaching for a pen, William's impatient face flashed on the screen. "Mia! Geez, I've been waiting for hours. Where's Dr. T.?"

She smiled, glad to see Jack's prodigy. Anything to distract her from her persistent anxiety. "I haven't seen him yet this morning."

"I have to ask him a question." He bounced in his excitement. "It's really important."

"I can get him for you." About to leave, she turned back, remembering what William had said on Sunday. "I don't suppose you figured out why I look so familiar to you."

He shook his head. "Not yet."

Thinking if she kept him talking, she might jog his memory, she asked, "Are you looking forward to Christmas tomorrow?"

He shrugged. "We're going to my aunt Debbie's. It's kinda boring, but the food's good." He launched into a detailed description of the day's usual menu.

What were Christmases like for her as a child? Were they big family events? Even though she couldn't recall, she felt melancholy at the thought of an uncelebrated Christmas.

An idea popped into her head, a way to eke a little joy out of the holiday. "William, can you help me out with something?" She told him what she needed and extracted a promise from him to send it to her.

"You gonna get Dr. T. now?" William asked, bouncing in his chair again.

"As soon as I set up the e-mail address where you can reach me. I promise. Just remember, it's a surprise."

Bringing up the browser on the laptop, she navigated to one of the free e-mail Web sites and created the address she'd given William. Then she hurried from the office, hoping to see Jack already up, pouring coffee in the kitchen. But the pot still sat untouched, the spice of cinnamon heavy in the air. She'd have to check his bedroom.

His door was shut. When she pressed her ear to the thick oak, she heard only silence from within. She knew she ought to walk away, tell William he'd have to wait a little longer to speak with Jack. But agitation pushed her to grab the doorknob. She turned it and eased the door open. Tipped her head inside.

Her breath caught in her throat at the sight of him sprawled facedown across his bed, blankets low on his hips, the sculptured lines of his body revealed from the waist up. The covers were twisted around his legs as if he'd had as bad a night as she had. Even in sleep his hands were tightened into fists, the tendons and muscles in his arms standing out in sharp relief.

Friday night their lovemaking had been so fierce, so quick, she'd had no time to touch him, to see him. To explore the texture of his skin along his rib cage, stroke the musculature along his back. She longed to do that now. To push back that long, black hair, rub her palm across his rough beard. To lie down beside him, her body stretched along his.

She stepped inside the room, crossing to the bed. William was waiting, no doubt growing more antsy by the minute. But she found herself sinking to the edge of the bed, sitting as softly as she could so as not to wake Jack.

As she watched him breathe, felt the warmth radiating from his skin, something stirred inside her, reaching into her heart. With each breath, that feeling grew within, enveloping her entire being. Emotions flooded her, so profound she could barely grasp everything she was feeling.

No. Don't even think it.

Despite her admonition, she felt a rush of hope, of joy rising up within herself like an electric shock. She knew she mustn't

let it into her conscious mind. She shouldn't think it, should-
n't acknowledge it, had to deny what she imagined she was
feeling. She barely knew this man, she hardly knew herself. As
seductive as those feelings were, they couldn't be real.

But I want so desperately to feel them.

He shifted, his hands opening and digging like claws into the
pillow. His breathing grew more rapid as he struggled against
some nightmare image. Her heart broke seeing his pain.

She laid her hand, featherlight, on his back. With a gasp,
he sat bolt upright, his eyes still clouded with sleep. His body
shook so violently she grabbed his hand to give him an anchor,
a way out of whatever darkness gripped him. He pulled her
up against him, his chest heaving, his skin fever hot.

His tremors faded as he held her. With her ear against his
chest, she could hear his heart racing, its rhythm breakneck.
He tugged her even closer, pushing the covers aside, his
erection thrusting against her. Forgetting why she'd come
into the room, forgetting even the bombshell that had tried to
force its way into her heart, she lifted her mouth to his.

As he kissed her, his mouth hot and wet on hers, he turned
her under him, pressing her back onto the bed. One hand
shoved her sweater up, the other fumbled with the button on
her jeans. She stroked him from his broad shoulders to his
hips, drawing her fingernails up again along his back. The
urgency to feel him inside her overwhelmed her.

He went suddenly still, his muscles rigid with tension.
Then, with a muttered oath he rolled from her. In one fluid
movement he was off the bed. He strode to the window and
leaned against the glass.

"Get out of the bed." He sucked in a breath. "Please. I don't
need any more damn temptation."

Shaking, she pulled her sweater down, rebuttoned her jeans. She backed toward the door, lingering there. His lean body was a work of art in the milky-white winter light. His erection drew her eye, kept her gaze riveted.

"What did you want?" he asked, dragging her attention up to his face.

For the first time, she saw the strain in him, as if he held on to civility by a slender thread. "William wants you. He said it was important."

He turned away slightly, concealing the evidence of his arousal. "Tell him I'll be there in a few minutes."

Sidling from the room, she returned to Jack's office. She relayed Jack's message to an impatient William, then checked her e-mail. William had already sent what he'd promised. She routed the attachment to Jack's printer, then found the sketch pad in the great room and tucked the printout inside.

She was relieved Jack hadn't yet emerged from his room. Grabbing his voluminous parka from the coat closet and sliding her feet into the oversize sneakers, she escaped outside.

It hadn't snowed for three days running now, but with the temperatures lingering below freezing, the blanket of white remained. Sullen gray clouds muted the sun, and the trees all wore thick clots of snow. Nothing but gray and white and black as far as the eye could see, all other color leached away.

His footprints from Friday night were partly filled in, but there were other, fresher tracks leading off between the trees. So the agony from Friday night hadn't been the last of it, just as he'd told her. He must have come out here during the night, leaving quietly enough that she hadn't heard him despite her own sleeplessness. If he'd shouted his anger, his grief, he'd muffled it somehow because she'd never heard a thing.

Moving carefully, placing her feet in his tracks, she followed his path. She nearly lost her balance more than once—his stride was far longer than hers—but she got as far as the trees. Her feet icy in the inadequate shoes, she gazed out into the monochromatic woods, trying to imagine his pain as he stood alone in the black night.

Her heart felt leaden in her chest at the thought of his solitude. But she doubted he would have let her comfort him if she'd been here with him.

"Mia!"

She turned at the still-foreign name to see him standing on the porch, shivering in the cold. He'd pushed his feet into boots, but she had his parka, so he had nothing but his flannel shirt to hold back the icy bite of the air. Even still, he steamrolled toward her, his face as moody as the cloudy sky.

"What the hell are you doing out here?" His breath roiling in the cold, he caught up to her. "Another storm is due in."

As if his words had triggered the clouds to let loose, a few small flakes of snow drifted down. Even without the science background tucked away in her reluctant brain, she could see the gray sky had darkened, foretelling a heavy snowfall.

Her feet nearly numb from the cold, she preceded him toward the house. "What did William want?"

"He just found out about a math camp for gifted students that runs during spring break. He needed a letter of reference. The deadline's not until mid-January, but he's afraid he won't be considered if he doesn't get the application in early."

She stepped back inside the house, grateful for the warmth. "You'll write it for him?"

He shoved his boots off and ordered her out of her shoes and the parka. As he hustled her toward the fire, he told her, "I e-mailed the organizer of the event. Let her know I'd pay for William's slot plus sponsor two others. And I'll write the letter."

They stood at the stove, Mia holding her hands as close as she could to the warmth. "He's lucky to have someone like you."

He didn't answer, his long hair hiding his face. Whatever nightmare had visited him in his sleep was still with him, holding him tight within its coils. The moments talking with William might have given Jack a brief respite, but the sunlight the boy might have shed had shut off like a sudden eclipse.

"Jack."

She put her hand on his arm. He walked away, stalking off across the great room and down the hall like a mountain lion, mortally wounded. His bedroom door slammed, an exclamation point to his rejection of her.

Her feet were moving before she worked out what she would say to him. She knocked on the door politely at first, then when he wouldn't respond, she pounded with her fist. "I'm not leaving, Jack. Let me in!"

She was ready to open the door and enter uninvited when she heard the latch give. His expression was anything but welcoming as he loomed over her.

Impulse had her pushing past him into the room. Memories of their lovemaking washed over her.

She wouldn't think about that. She turned toward him, arms crossed over her middle. "Talk to me, Jack. Let me help you."

"This isn't something you can fix, Mia."

"At least let me be with you."

He approached her with a glance down at the bed. "Not a good idea."

"Jack…" She lifted her hand to his face, rested her palm against his cheek. For a moment, his rigid jaw softened, and she thought he would yield his secrets to her.

Then he wrenched away, breaking the contact. Turned his back to her. "I don't want you here, Mia."

She couldn't leave it at that. She reached out for him again, fingers barely brushing against his shoulder. He turned, expression fierce, flinging her hand away. "Leave me the hell alone!"

The force of his anger sent her stumbling backward against the dresser. She heard a crash, glanced over at the highboy to see a framed picture had toppled. When Jack reached toward her, she shrank back, suddenly terrified by what that large hand might do to her.

"Please don't," she pleaded, the words seeming to come from someone else. Her heart raced even as she saw Jack was only righting the photo. The wedding picture she'd seen in the guest room.

He stood motionless, hand still on the highboy as he watched her. But as she watched, his face and his body seemed to change, as if someone else's image overlaid his. She saw hands in fists, a face twisted with rage. A monster's eyes burning her as blows rained down.

"Mia?"

A roaring in her ears muted Jack's voice. Thrust into a maelstrom of fear, she collapsed inward on herself, falling to the floor. Arms over her head to protect herself, she sobbed and screamed as she prayed for the agony to be over.

His first touch on her arm bludgeoned her, although some small scrap of her mind understood it was the barest brushing of fingertips. He murmured her name over and over again, then endearments that finally grabbed at her heart and pulled her from her waking nightmare. She let him tug her into his arms, burrowing against his flannel shirt.

She didn't know how long they sat there. At one point he

repositioned himself, leaning against the bed and pulling her into his lap. Where before her confused mind had felt punishment from him, now she only felt comfort.

His breath ruffled her hair. "Focus on yourself, Mia. Not me."

"But I care about you." It was more than that, but she wasn't about to explore those feelings.

He eased her away from him. "Don't care, Mia. It's a waste of time." He rose, then helped her to her feet.

At the door she turned back. "I thought I'd make chili for dinner."

"I won't be joining you."

She nodded and walked away, feeling bereft. As she forced herself to keep moving, resisting the temptation to look back, the door latched quietly behind her.

He followed a ritual on Christmas Eve. At three o'clock in the afternoon, he was seven hours into it, building up the rage and grief that would peak at 8:21 p.m. To the hour and minute when he found Elizabeth.

Unlike Mia and her well-meaning interruptions, Dawson knew well enough to stay out of Jack's life from December twenty-third through the twenty-fifth. Dawson shielded him from outsiders even more thoroughly this time of year, telling anyone who asked that Jack took an annual ski trip to Park City every Christmas.

William, of course, knew nothing. Jack had only been mentoring the boy for six months, hadn't had to deal with the brilliant, cheerful prodigy during the Christmas holiday. Wouldn't have had to today if he'd remembered to shut down his computer before bed. But after standing in the icy darkness last night until he was nearly numb from cold, he'd headed straight to his room and the blast of a hot shower, computer forgotten.

Still, those few moments with William had briefly lit the dank cave Jack inhabited this time of year. Gave him something to think about besides his grief.

Why, then, was William welcome as a distraction but Mia was not? He knew at least one reason, although he could guess at a couple more if he were willing to be honest with himself. Mia reminded him of the happiness he once had and could never have again. Just her presence here in his home dragged bare emotions into the open, exposing him to more pain.

Outside his bedroom window, thick snow obliterated the view of the trees. The heavy cloud cover had squelched the sun, casting a dim, gray pall over the landscape. The world outside seemed to grow smaller and smaller with each storm, until there was nothing but this house and him and Mia inside it.

Mia's presence confronted him with an uncomfortable truth—that he indulged himself with his grief, that he wallowed in it. As horrifying as Elizabeth's death had been, it was five years past. Wasn't it time he put it away, stuffed it in a box somewhere out of sight?

If only he could pull this knife out of his gut so easily. His psychologist wife would have labeled it post-traumatic stress disorder, would have recommended counseling. He'd seen a therapist, but it had only been a half-assed attempt. There were too damn many locked doors he'd just as soon not pry open with the process.

Which brought his mind back around to Mia and her talent for wielding an emotional crowbar. It wasn't intentional. She'd asked few questions, had left his past alone for the most part. But she had only to stand in the same room with him to flay him with her sweetness, her caring.

He could just take her to his bed, bury his nightmares that way. It was what his body had been clamoring for since Friday night. Why not use sex to sublimate the pain?

The thought of using Mia that way sickened him. Especially since he sensed that their lovemaking had meant far more to her than it had to him. Women couldn't help responding that way to intimacy. And Mia was even more vulnerable than most.

A tantalizing fragrance worked its way into his room— onions and spices, the beginnings of chili. Was she making the promised meal just for herself? Or did she have hopes it would lure him out of his room? It damn well might. The aroma had set off a rumbling in his stomach. The hunger was a revelation; he'd had little appetite in the past few days.

Her quiet rap on his door set off a jangling in every nerve ending. For a heartbeat he considered ignoring her, but his feet were moving toward the threshold in the next instant.

As the door swung open, he tried to brace himself for the sight of her. His heart slammed in his chest as she tipped her serious face up to him, the cheery snowman on her red sweater grinning in counterpoint.

"I was looking for beans for the chili."

He edged past her. "There are some staples stored on a shelf in the garage."

She followed him down the hall, through the kitchen, to the garage. He indicated the shelf above the chest freezer. "I keep the pantry overflow here."

Going up on tiptoe, she reached for a can of black beans at the back of the shelf, her fingertips barely brushing the can. Stretching past her, his body arching over hers, he took down two cans and set them on the freezer.

And should have moved away. Stepped back and waited while she took the cans into the house. Except she didn't take them and he stayed put, close enough to hear her breath, to inhale her scent, to feel her warmth curling from her body. He might as well be a magnet the way he leaned even closer to her.

She still had her back to him, but had lowered her arm and curved ever so slightly toward him. Her head bent down, exposing even more of her slender throat. The ends of her dark hair lay in stark contrast to her pale skin. There was no resisting the urge to kiss her.

In the chill of the garage, the back of her neck was hot against his mouth. He wondered if the source of her scent was here or at her throat or in her hair. Between her breasts, along her hips, between her legs. He went hard at the thought of exploring each part of her body in his pursuit of that elusive fragrance.

His hands around her waist, he pulled her back, and her body molded against his. His fingers dipped beneath her red sweater, then tugged her T-shirt free of her jeans. The jeans were loose enough that he could easily slide his hand inside and past the elastic waistband of her panties.

She shivered. Mouth close to her ear, he whispered, "Too cold?" In response, she reached back with her hand, wedging it between their bodies, fingers spread across his erection. He nearly went to his knees from the pressure.

Leaning against the freezer, he stroked Mia's flat belly, reveling in the feel of her satiny skin. With each pass, he dipped lower until he brushed the soft curls below. Mia pressed harder against the front of his jeans, the heel of her hand moving along his length.

He wanted everything at once—his mouth on her everywhere, his body buried deep inside hers. The feel of her climaxing against his hand. He wanted to devour her, pull her inside him, keep her forever safe.

As he couldn't Elizabeth. The sudden intrusion sent a chill through him, momentarily stilled the movement of his hand. He pushed away the unwanted thought, squeezed his eyes shut more tightly, closing out everything but Mia and the feel of her in his arms.

With hasty greed, he thrust his fingers between Mia's soft folds, seeking out her hot, sensitive center. Her legs gave way, but he supported her, his free arm hooked around her waist. He drove his finger inside her, the wet warmth nearly pushing him over the edge. Then he rubbed her with slow strokes of his palm, feeling her vibrate against him.

She came with a guttural cry, her body growing heavier as she melted in his arms. He thrust inside her again, felt her flex around his fingers as she climaxed again. The honeyed wetness against his hand sent his heart rate screaming.

She twisted in his arms, pulling free to face him. "I want you inside me." She reached for his fly, had it half down before he stopped her.

"Condoms are inside," he reminded her.

She took his hand, pulling him along behind her. At that moment he would have followed her outside to make love in the snow.

The house phone was ringing when they stepped inside. He ignored it, letting her tow him through the kitchen, toward the hall. The answering machine clicked on to pick up the call.

The sound of William's tearful voice stopped him in his tracks. "Dr. T.? Are you there? Please—" He broke off with sob. "Something happened to my mom."

Chapter Twelve

While Jack retreated to his office to speak with William, Mia returned for the black beans she'd abandoned. Her body still vibrated in reaction to what had happened in the garage, but she was aching for more. Her emotions were scattered across the map, muddling her mind, leaving her with barely enough brain power to finish putting together dinner.

She drained the beans then threw them into the pot with the rest of the chili makings. The scent of cumin and chili powder swirled off the surface as she stirred, mingling with just a hint of cinnamon. Her impulse to sprinkle in that spice had surprised her. She could only guess it was her secret ingredient for chili.

Covering the pot again, she started opening cupboards in search of cornmeal for corn bread. Jack kept flour and sugar in canisters on the counter; she'd found those when she'd made muffins. She finally located the cornmeal in the pantry on the next-to-top shelf.

As she used the stepstool to reach the bag, she spotted a box of the cinnamon herb tea she'd enjoyed Sunday night. She made a mental note to have some after dinner. Maybe it would soothe her into sleep.

She measured the dry ingredients into a bowl for the corn bread and checked on the supply of eggs and milk. It was early yet, not quite four o'clock. She wouldn't finish the corn bread for another couple hours.

She stepped from the kitchen and around the corner toward Jack's office. His voice rumbled through the shut door, but she couldn't make out what he was saying. Anxiety for William prickled along her skin.

At a loss for what else to do, she wiped down the already clean counters and wet mopped the floor. She'd planned to prepare the chili toppings later, but needing to keep busy, she went ahead and chopped onions, sliced black olives and grated some sharp cheddar.

Jack finally entered the kitchen just as Mia was setting the washed grater in the dish drainer. His expression told her nothing as he leaned against the counter, arms crossed over his chest.

"Well?" she asked, wringing the kitchen towel in her hands.

"His mom passed out at work. He and the neighbor weren't notified until this morning—William spends the night at a neighbor's while his mom works and it took some time to find that contact number."

"Is she going to be okay?"

"I spoke to the neighbor. Apparently Mrs. Franklin has high blood pressure. She should be fine with medication."

Relief flooded her. "How's William doing?"

"Shook up. Scared to death. I told him and the neighbor if there was anything she needed medically I'd make sure she got it."

Of course he would. She'd seen how he felt about William despite the short time he'd known the boy. Because he cared about William, because the boy meant so much to him, Jack's generosity would know no bounds. What would it be like if he felt that way about her?

Longing stabbed her, that she could be as important to him. That he would feel more for her than compassion toward a stranger. That there would be more to the connection between them than simple physical attraction.

He crossed to the refrigerator and took out a bottle of water. "I got a call on the business line while I was talking to William's neighbor. Dawson."

Mia could think of only one reason Jack would bring up his conversation with Dawson. "What did he say?"

"He finally managed to line up a crew to clear the road. They won't be able to start until after Christmas, of course, but the road should be open in less than a week. Assuming the weather clears like the forecasts are promising."

"That's good." It was, wasn't it? To be able to leave here, try to find a way back to her life? Why, then, did it feel as if a rock had settled in her stomach?

And why did Jack look as grim as if he'd just delivered the worst news of all?

While Jack spent the next two hours hashing out the details involving Mrs. Franklin's care, Mia took her drawing pad into her room. Using the printout from William, she sketched until her hand cramped and the light outside faded completely to black. Shaking the constriction from her hand, she studied her work and decided she was happy with the result. She tore the sheet carefully from the pad and rolled it up, using some purple yarn she found in the closet to tie it.

At a quarter to six, with no sign of Jack, she threw the corn bread together and set the pan of batter in the oven. Listening for him as she washed the mixing bowl and measuring cups, she realized she might be eating alone. Ignoring a pang of loneliness, she pulled down bowls and plates for two. Cheese, onions, olives and sour cream set out, she waited for the corn bread to bake.

The timer beeped on the oven just as Jack appeared, sleeves of his wool flannel shirt rolled up and his hair mussed as if he'd been running his fingers through it. Seeing him, she couldn't hold back a spurt of joy.

Mitts on, she slid out the hot corn bread. As she set the pan on the granite countertop, he shut the oven door for her.

"Dinner's ready," she told him. She held her breath, hoping he would say he'd join her, steeling herself for the possibility he wouldn't.

He shut off the stove, shoved his hands in his pockets. He looked from the steaming corn bread to the large pot of chili on the stove. "I'm starving." He seemed surprised.

She handed him a bowl, then fished a ladle out of a drawer. He dipped it deep into the pot of chili, then brought up a generous helping. He filled the bowl, exchanging it with the empty one. Mia cut the corn bread and put the hot squares into the bread basket.

They sat at the dining-room table, the pellet stove adding a flickering orange warmth from the adjacent great room. After sprinkling cheese and onions on his chili, Jack picked up his spoon and gazed down at the steaming bowl.

"Thank you for making dinner tonight. It's not something I usually do on Christmas Eve."

She scooped up a cheese-laden spoonful. "I wanted a special meal for the holiday."

He took a bite, then sighed with pleasure. "Chili seems like an unusual choice for Christmas."

"Now that you mention it…" She swirled sour cream through the dark red mixture. "When I first thought of making chili, I wasn't making a connection between it and Christmas Eve. But it seems right. As if it's a traditional meal for me."

"You mentioned Arizona. Maybe it's something people do in the southwest." He heaped another mouthful on his spoon. "In any case, it's delicious."

Jack went for a second helping. The bright orange shreds of cheddar he dropped into his bowl relaxed onto the hot surface. That was how she had felt when he'd stroked her, melting against his body.

She shook off the image. "Did you get everything settled with William's mom?"

"Her medical insurance only covered a fraction of her hospital stay and none of her prescriptions. I told her I'd make up any shortfall."

"You're a good man, Jack."

He shrugged off her compliment. "She needed a hand. I gave it to her."

"Not everyone would."

"No," he said quietly. "They wouldn't."

Done with her chili, Mia drizzled honey on her corn bread, licking the stickiness from her fingers when she'd eaten the last bit. She felt Jack's gaze on her and shivered when she saw the heat in his eyes. A throbbing started up between her legs, her body remembering his clever fingers touching her, thrusting inside.

He rose abruptly, shoving back his chair. With a clatter, he tossed his spoon into his empty bowl. "Done?" he asked as he reached for her dishes. She nodded and he stacked them with hers.

She brought in the rest of the corn bread and wrapped it for the freezer. Once Jack was finished with their few dishes, he held open plastic zipper bags while she ladled portions of leftover chili into them.

As they worked, an awareness sparked between them, crackling along Mia's skin. His hands brushed against her, contact that could have been accidental, except his fingers would linger. When she glanced up at him, his gaze would be on her mouth or the line of her throat. She could almost feel his lips pressed there.

Then he seemed to take a step back, breaking eye contact entirely. He turned his back to her as he washed the chili pot, walking away without a word to carry the leftovers to the garage freezer. A battle seemed to rage inside him between approach and retreat. Mia only knew she wanted him to wrap her in his arms.

He took his time in the garage. Mia swiped the counters clean one last time, then tried to figure out what to do next. She felt ready to explode, emotions tumbling and bursting from inside her. She needed some resolution from Jack, but she wasn't sure what that should be.

Her gaze fell on the teakettle on the back of the stove. A cup of cinnamon tea might not settle her, but preparing it would at least give her something to do with her hands. Filling the kettle, she set it on the gas to heat, then pulled the step stool up to the pantry cabinet.

Climbing to the top step, she scanned the contents of the top shelf for any hidden treasures she might be able to use for a Christmas dinner. Poking her head inside, she spotted a can of cranberry sauce tucked behind a palisade of soup cans. When she reached for it, she upset an open tin. Cinnamon sticks spilled onto the shelf, their aroma blasting her.

Her mind clouded, she swayed on the step stool. Felt herself falling into space as images pummeled her. A fist slamming against her face, punching her chest. A boot against her ribs.

She floated away, hovering over herself, watching an enraged man beat her. Except it wasn't *her* enduring the man's wrath. It was a four-year-old girl cowering and screaming and begging Daddy to stop.

And everywhere, the scent of cinnamon, like a thick, choking smog. Pain and cinnamon locked together in her mind. Punishing fists and that spicy scent now bitter on her tongue.

"Mia!"

The syllables meant nothing to her; they were nothing but nonsense noise. She was too busy watching the little girl curled up on herself like a pill bug, trying to be small enough to evade the blows.

"Mia!"

The voice was louder now. Something, someone shook her. With a jolt she crashed back into her body, not the little girl's but her own. One last scream escaped from that tortured child through Mia's own mouth as she suddenly came to from her waking nightmare.

For an instant it was a monster's face bent over her, the rage of her unknown attacker distilled into a demon's visage. She struggled against the constraint of his arms, mad with terror. Then Jack's voice registered in her ears, Jack's firm but gentle touch, and she collapsed against him.

She shuddered as powerfully as she had that first day when he'd saved her from the creek, except it wasn't bone-deep cold that shook her body. Burrowing against his chest, eyes closed, she inhaled the clean scent of him, the faint trace of cinnamon dispersing.

He rose, lifting her in his arms, carrying her to the great room. Easing into the recliner, he nestled her in his lap, curved one hand against her cheek. His hand felt cool where he traced soothing circles on her skin. The rest of him felt warm and rock steady, a bulwark against the black unknown concealed inside her.

She clutched his shirt to keep him near. "You saved me again."

"I heard you screaming." He kissed her brow. "You were toppling off the ladder when I came in."

She took an uneven breath. "Another flashback. I was looking for something in the cupboard. I smelled cinnamon…"

"Scent can be a powerful trigger."

"But this time…" She struggled to make sense of what she'd seen. "I saw a little girl." Her head swung up as realization struck. "It was me. As a child. Being beaten." The last word came out in a rasping whisper.

The motion of his hand stilled. "Who beat you?"

"I think it was my father." Her throat closing with remembered fear, she described the scene she'd seen in her mind's eye. "Is that what my memory loss is all about, then? My father beat me as a child and I'm still traumatized by it?" She shook her head even as she said it. "That makes no sense."

She did know with gut-level certainty that the little girl

she'd seen was her. But she could muster no sense of peril surrounding her father.

Jack stroked her back. "You're safe now," he murmured.

The touch of his fingers distracted her from her contemplation. "I'll always feel safe with you."

A mix of emotions played across his face—guilt, uneasiness, longing. "Don't count too much on me, Mia."

She took his face in her hands, his rough beard prickling against her palms. "I'll take whatever you can give me."

He wrapped his fingers around her wrists and tugged them away. But he didn't let go. "I can't give you anything but my body."

"That's enough," she said, even as despair settled in her chest.

"I can't, Mia." The edginess was back in his eyes.

"Because of your wife."

"Yes. No." He turned away, the fire casting shadows on his face. "There's something building inside me. Call it my own flashback. Memories of that night she died, but more than that."

"But wouldn't it be easier to be with me?"

"Dammit! Of course it would!" He let go of her, digging the heels of his hands into his eyes. When he dropped his hands again, his eyes blazed with a dark fire. "I can't use you that way."

He shifted, pushing away from her, leaving her on the chair as he prowled before the fire. "It plays over and over in my mind, each time more vivid, more real. From the first of December until now. Until the time she died."

"When?" she asked, barely able to push out the question.

"Eight twenty-one." His head jerked toward the clock that hung above the pellet stove. "An hour and a half from now. I see myself coming home...finding her..."

He lunged at her, hands propped on the arms of the recliner, trapping her. "If I take you into my bedroom now, it will be nothing but sex, Mia. Nothing but a way to drive the ugliness from my mind."

She flinched at his raw declaration. Wanted to deny what he was telling her. She saw the wildness in his eyes, the corded muscles in his arms. Everything about him was hard, taut, as if it took every last scrap of his will to keep from self-destructing.

And yet…she remembered the longing she'd seen in his face. Could see a fragment of it still, almost pleading with her to say yes. Maybe she was only fooling herself, was only seeing what she wanted to see. But instinct told her that despite what he'd said, he yearned for more.

"I want to be whatever you need tonight." She wouldn't think about why, wasn't ready to let that thought in.

He stared at her for a long moment, his gaze hotter than the flames flickering in the stove. "Why couldn't you leave me alone?" he rasped out.

He lifted her again, carrying her from the great room and down the hall. The air should have felt cooler away from the fire, but Jack felt as hot as a furnace, as if his tension converted to heat as he kicked open his bedroom door and slammed it shut again. He set her on the bed gently enough, but then stripped the comforter out from under her.

"Take off your clothes," he told her as his fingers went to the buttons on his shirt. Illuminated by the bedside lamp, he was all rough angles, light and shadow.

She tugged her sweater and T-shirt off in one motion, enjoying the way his hand fumbled when he saw her bared breasts. Unashamed, she pushed off her jeans and panties, moving aside as he lay beside her, naked, on the bed.

Reaching into the drawer, he tossed a handful of condoms on top of the nightstand. She thought he would sheathe himself, immediately plunge inside her. She wanted that as much as he did, wanted to be joined with him, one with him. The need rippling off him stoked her own.

But instead he stretched out beside her. Drew his hand leisurely along her body from shoulder to hip. Pressed soft kisses on her mouth, her cheek, her jaw. Traced the whorls of her ear with the tip of his tongue. His tenderness melted her heart even as it heated her body.

She couldn't lie still. She threw one leg over him, wanting his thick heat inside her, but he nudged her back, flat on the bed. He continued his gentle assault with his hand, stroking in growing circles from rib cage to belly, then higher, lower with each arc.

The first brush of his hand against her soft curls, she strangled back a cry. He moved in slow motion back up, just to the bottom of her breasts. Her nipples stood out hard and aching for his touch. But still, he teased her, so very close yet not quite reaching his goal.

When he again passed the nest of curls, she grabbed his wrist, desperate for his touch on her sensitized flesh. She hadn't the strength to force his hand and glared up at him in frustration. His mouth curved into a smile, and with his hot gaze on her, he bowed his head and drew her nipple into his mouth.

A low, guttural moan slipped from her throat. His teeth grazed her nipple, sending heat zinging from her breasts to the vee of her legs. Again it was impossible to lie still, her legs moving restlessly. Her fingers holding his wrist grew lax, allowing him to resume his unhurried exploration of her body.

When finally he parted her folds, trailed his fingertip along her sensitive nub, a lightning bolt of sensation struck. Then he thrust a finger inside her, and she climaxed, crying out in ecstatic surprise. As her body clenched around his finger, she clutched his wrist again to hold him there.

A last circling of her nipple with his tongue, then he moved to her mouth, kissing her softly, taking his time. She could feel his erection, as hard as stone against her thigh, the tip wetting her skin. But he still didn't reach for a condom. Instead he lay on his back and pulled her toward him.

"Straddle me," he whispered.

When she tried to sit across his hips, he stopped her. Gaze locked with hers, he urged her higher until she was positioned at his shoulders, knees beside his head, facing the carved oak headboard. The curls between her legs shivered with each breath he exhaled.

"Hold on," he murmured, and she did, wrapping her fingers around the headboard.

Then he lifted his mouth to her.

The first touch of his tongue ran through her like a shock and she was grateful for the anchor of the headboard. Her fingers dug into the wood, bliss running through her at the wet slide of his tongue. She couldn't hold back the explosion, felt it thunder through her like a rockslide. Flung to pieces like that crumbling mountainside, she drifted into an exquisite emptiness.

Drowsy and sated, she all but slumped to the bed when he released her hips. He gazed at her lying beside him, an intense light in his eyes. There was still tension in his face, a tautness she knew she could soothe with her body. He'd said this would mean nothing more to him than physical release, yet he'd delayed his pleasure for so long to give her hers.

She pressed her hand to his cheek, a brightness welling up

inside her. Still unwilling to accept the message her heart was sending, she forced herself to remain silent. Soon enough she would have to deal with the emotional fallout in the aftermath. For now this would be the only gift he would take from her.

Reaching across him, she took a condom from the night-stand and ripped it open. He didn't stop her as she took his erection in her hand, his sharp intake of breath the only sign of the strain he was under. As she unrolled the condom, his fingers dug into the mattress, tendons popping out on his hands.

When he made to rise, she pressed his shoulders back into the bed. She straddled his body again, this time across his hips. Taking his hard flesh in her hand, she eased him inside her, watching his face as each inch slipped deeper.

He pulled her down, gathering her close. Mouth close to her ear, he murmured her name, whispered endearments. None of them promises, none of them meant for anywhere but this bed. But she took them into her heart nonetheless.

He lay motionless as she cradled him inside her, his large hands spread across her back, their heat seeping into her. Then with his mouth on hers, his tongue dipping inside, he cocked his hips up toward her. She pressed down as he moved up, their rhythm in perfect synchronicity.

Then his thrusts increased in tempo, losing their grace, even as pleasure lapped at her again. His tongue plunged deeply in tandem with his hot flesh, giving her more of him with each stroke. He climaxed, his deep groan matching hers as she came again, astonished by the shattering sensations. Her body squeezed him over and over, as if it would not will-ingly release him from its domain.

Finally she slid from him, her head pillowed on his arm, her body curved tightly against his. She mustered the energy to tug the comforter over them both, then relaxed against him, listening to his slowing heart.

And felt her lies come crashing down on her. That she could deal with the emotional fallout. That she could be intimate with him without wanting more. That he was a stranger who meant nothing more to her than someone who gave her shelter. And the most monumental lie—that she could leave him and still remain whole.

Then came the next rockslide, the biggest one of all. The one she could no longer hold back, no longer ignore.

I love him.

She lay there, stunned, afraid to look up at him, terrified of what he might see in her face. Fearful that he could somehow feel it in the way her body lay against his, the way her heart beat, her breath moved in and out of her lungs.

She loved him. With all his edges, all his secrets. She loved him as she had never loved—

A name skittered across her conscious mind then vanished. A chill crept over her skin despite the comforter and Jack's warm body beside her.

She had loved someone before. Or thought she did. If she cared for someone as much as she did Jack, how could she have possibly forgotten? Of all the things her mind might have wanted to conceal, why would it have hidden love?

It must be someone in her past, someone no longer in her life. She had only the impression that there had been someone once, not that that someone was still a part of her world.

With Jack's breathing growing slower, deeper, she took a chance, looking up at him. His eyes were closed, his body so relaxed it was obvious he was asleep. The demons that had been pursuing him all day, all week, had given up the chase.

Lifting her head high enough to see, Mia checked the clock. Ten to eight. She settled her head back against Jack's arm to wait.

An hour later, when 8:21 p.m. had come and gone, Jack still slept. Mia closed her eyes, as well, and let herself drift off into dreams.

Chapter Thirteen

Jack's eyes snapped open. Light poured in through the bedroom window, the warm yellow of sunshine rather than the milky white of overcast skies. The bed beside him was empty, but he could still feel Mia's warmth on the sheets.

Then it hit him with the force of a sledgehammer. He'd slept through zero hour. Had damn near slept through the night for the first time in weeks. He'd woken only once, at 2:00 or 3:00 a.m., he wasn't sure. He'd reached for Mia and they'd made love, both of them half-asleep but hungry for each other. The feel of his climax still tingled along his nerve endings.

Had he used a condom? A quick glance at the nightstand told him there were two empty packets. He huffed with relief. Bad enough he'd used Mia the way he had. To have risked making her pregnant when she would soon be out of his life would have been beyond wrong.

And she would be leaving. In several days, a week, however long it would take the crew Dawson hired to plow through the snow and dig out the rockslide. And once the road was clear, he'd transport Mia to the county sheriff and watch her walk out of his life.

Better it happened sooner than later. The longer she stayed, the more he could fool himself into thinking she belonged here. She had a whole other life out there, one that she would no doubt be glad to return to once she regained her memories.

And he'd be alone again. Which would be better for both of them. She didn't fit into his life. He'd worked hard to carve out a space for his isolation, a way to live with Elizabeth's death and everything that had followed. Mia had let him forget for a little while, had given him safe passage through the anniversary. But that wasn't something he should be depending on.

He ran his hand over the place where she'd slept, only a trace of her body heat left on the sheets. Soon it would be as cold as it always was in this bed. He'd gotten used to that once before, when Elizabeth died. He hardly thought anymore about the emptiness of a solitary bed. Even if Mia joined him here again, he'd have to keep reminding himself her stay was only temporary.

Tossing aside the comforter, he pushed to his feet and headed for the bathroom, snagging a clean pair of boxers on his way. When he stepped back into the bedroom a few minutes later, the aroma of coffee drifted in through the partly open door. A quick glance told him she'd grabbed only her sweater before leaving.

He'd taken a step toward the door to go after her when it swung open and she edged inside with two mugs of coffee. As she walked past him to set a mug on the nightstand, he breathed in her enigmatic fragrance and caught a glimpse of pale, silky skin below the hem of her red sweater.

She sat cross-legged on her side of the bed, mug cradled in her hands. "Two sugars, right?"

What the hell did he care what was in his coffee when she sat there in his bed? But she'd made the effort to remember how he liked it, had brought him a cup. He took a sip of the scalding brew, set the cup down again. "It's fine."

She smiled, temptation in a slender, intriguingly scented package. The best Christmas gift he could possibly imagine.

Her smile faded as he hooked his thumbs in his boxers and slid them off. Hand trembling she set the coffee aside on the nightstand, a few drops of coffee sloshing on her skin.

When her gaze dropped to his erection, he felt himself grow even harder. Then she reached out for him and welcomed him into her arms.

She lost count of the number of times they made love. When the handful of condoms he'd set on the nightstand ran out, he suggested other ways to pleasure each other both rather than reach into the box for more. Their coffee grew cold on the nightstands as Jack explored a dozen ways to drive her wild.

They showered together, Jack soaping her body, the feel of his hands pushing her over the edge again. She returned the favor, her fingers circling the hot hard length of him until he reached completion under the warm shower spray.

When they finally emerged from the bedroom, Mia's muscles ached, but her skin glowed with remembered sensation. In the kitchen she threw together a batch of banana muffins while Jack whipped up omelets.

But as they ate together at the breakfast bar, Jack seemed

to shut down, bit by bit. Close himself off from her. As if he had second thoughts about what had happened in his bedroom, as if he worried that their lovemaking had meant more to her than he'd intended it to.

Of course it had. Each time they'd made love had only confirmed her love for him, anchored it that much more deeply in her heart. Despite the hopelessness of it, the impossibility of any life with him, during the past twenty-four hours she'd only come to love him more.

With that realization, despair settled like a rock in her stomach. What was she going to do when the road was cleared? When she had no more justification for being with him?

He'd promised her nothing. She had no reason to expect anything from him. Even now he wouldn't look at her, and she could read regret in every line of his body.

She had to say something, had to find a way to hold on to those intimate hours with him. "Jack?"

"I'll clean up." He all but jumped to his feet, gathering the dishes and carrying them to the sink.

His broad back turned toward her, a formidable barrier as he shut her out. Emotion ambushed her, tightening the back of her throat.

She fought to keep her voice steady. "I think I need to lie down." She hurried from the kitchen.

In the guest room, her back pressed against the closed door, she let the tears go. They soaked her face, wet her hands as she pressed them to her cheeks. This was the aftermath she'd sworn she could handle, the lie she'd so easily let herself believe. And part of that lie was her conviction that somehow Jack would come to love her as she loved him.

She shivered, the coolness of the room chilling her. She'd

been so warm after her shower she'd pulled on only a T-shirt. Now she wanted her sweater but had left it behind in Jack's room.

She could just grab another sweater or one of the sweatshirts Jack had given her from the dresser drawer. But the red sweater with its snowman and Christmas-tree decoration was the only thing from her forgotten life that had any meaning for her. Right now she needed the comfort of that dim familiarity.

When she made her way down the hall, Jack's office door was shut and she could hear the rumble of his voice as he spoke on the phone. She quickly crossed the great room toward the master suite, then scanned the room for her sweater. She spotted it at the foot of the highboy where Jack had tossed it when she'd brought them coffee earlier.

She pulled it on and hugged herself, willing her memories to return. It was a useless effort; her mind was as empty as it had been since she'd arrived in Jack's woods. Only a few disparate bits of information knocked around in her potholed brain, nothing she could hang a life on.

Her gaze fell on the wedding photo of Jack and Elizabeth. She took it down, seating herself on the foot of the bed. The happiness on Jack's face filled her with joy and longing in equal measure. If he would only smile at her like that, even once, it would be enough.

A faint scent of cinnamon drifted toward her, likely from the coffee that still sat, cold, on the nightstands. She remembered sprinkling cinnamon on the grounds before she'd started the brew cycle. Cinnamon, like the tea, like the sticks she'd upset in the cupboard. She'd put it in the spice muffins she'd made last week, had almost spooned some in the banana muffins.

The spiciness tugged at her, fogged her mind. Her hand holding the photo shook, the image seeming to scramble, rearrange itself. Her gaze fixed on Jack's face as it changed, morphed into something different, darker. His smile froze into a grimace of rage and she shrank back from it, dropping the photo on the floor.

Fragments of memory ripped through her mind, puzzle pieces in a whirlwind, passing by too quickly to grasp. One by one the pieces coalesced, overlaying a new image on top of the one lying at her feet. She saw the new photograph in a flash of recollection, and the story she'd read years ago was suddenly fresh in her mind. A woman beaten to death. Her husband arrested for her murder.

The woman was Elizabeth. Jack was her husband.

Horror welled up in her, grabbed her by the throat. At first she couldn't make a sound, could barely breathe. Then terror punched out a scream that all but deafened her. She stood there, frozen, the noise of her own fear horrible to her own ears.

Then the monster burst into the room and she tried to run, slamming into the windowed wall, jamming herself into a corner. When he tried to grab her, she punched and kicked at him, crazed, insane with fear. She only knew that if he caught her, he'd beat her like he did his wife, kill her, too.

Then his arms were around her, holding hers in place. His legs across hers to hold them down. She sobbed and screamed until her throat was raw, then quieted into whimpers. Only then could she hear his voice, soft, soothing.

"Honey, sweetheart." His murmur sifted into her ears like a balm. "Shh, quiet, love. You're safe. You're safe."

She forced out a few rasping words. "Can't let you."

"Can't let me what, sweetheart?"

"Can't let you touch me."

He kissed her, the brush of his mouth so gentle. Her heart ached with love for him. "Why not, love? Why shouldn't I touch you?"

"Because…" She steeled herself against the softness spreading inside her. "Because you killed her."

Ice filled his veins, and Jack's body went rigid. He swallowed back the compulsion to run, to leave Mia in here to battle her own demons. Where the hell he'd go, he had no idea. Out to freeze to death in the woods maybe, anything to not have to face Mia's accusation.

But he stayed. "I didn't kill anyone, Mia."

She was shaking again, and he released her long enough to pull the comforter from his bed. She didn't move. He supposed that was a good sign; maybe she was coming to her senses. Or maybe she was just catatonic.

Sitting beside her again, he threw the comforter over them both. To his everlasting gratitude, she didn't bolt. But he could feel the tension in every line of her body.

"How did your wife die?" The words came out in a whisper.

All this time she'd never asked him. He gave her the bald truth. "An intruder broke into our apartment and beat her to death."

"An intruder." There wasn't a shred of accusation in her tone, but his mind put it there, anyway.

"A meth addict, Reggie Phillips. There was a dealer in the complex next door to ours. Phillips got them mixed up."

"But they arrested *you*."

An iron weight dropped in the pit of his stomach at the memory. "Before they found Phillips. *He's* the one they convicted."

She drew back from him, turning, a light of recognition in her eyes. "I remember. I read about it in the papers. On the Internet." Her brow furrowed. "I read everything I could about the story."

The weight in his stomach grew heavier. "Then maybe you can explain to me," he said bitterly, "why the hell everyone thought I owed them every damned detail of my life."

She blushed. "I swear, it wasn't like that. It wasn't you I wanted to know about as much as her. Because of what had happened to me."

"Because your father beat you."

She shuddered, reaching for his hand. "I didn't like how obsessed I became with your wife's story. I forced myself to stop reading around the time you were acquitted."

"Not acquitted. The charges were dropped." He fixed his gaze on her, wanting to be sure she understood.

Her fingers laced more tightly with his. "It must have been so horrible for you."

Mia's words echoed in his mind, a sense of déjà vu rolling over him. Joanna Sanchez had said nearly the same thing to him to induce him to spill his guts to her.

The walls he'd slowly let down over the past week and a half slammed back into place. "Fishing for details?"

The confusion in Mia's face seemed real. "Of what?"

"Of what she looked like when I found her. The mess the apartment was in. The way I slipped in her blood on the kitchen floor."

The color drained from her face and her hand grew lax in his. "I don't…please…"

With a shock he realized she was about to pass out from his graphic description. Not the reaction he'd come to expect from the ghouls like Joanna who had hounded him five years ago.

Guilt goaded him into pulling her toward him again. "I'm a damned idiot. I'm sorry."

She leaned against him, the small tremors running through her body slowly quieting. "I'm sorry she died in such a terrible way."

Her words poured over him like a soothing balm. For the first time since his ineffectual sessions with a therapist, he wanted to talk about what had happened. Not the worst of the horror—he'd have to spare Mia that. But if he could just talk it out, maybe he could dull the images that still lay in his mind, as sharp as broken crystal.

He shut his eyes, her warmth enfolding him. "I was dead tired that night. I'd spent three days at a conference, then three more visiting my sister for an early Christmas."

Her nod against his chin invited him to continue. "Elizabeth and I had fought a few days earlier when I'd called her from Seattle. We hadn't quite smoothed it over before I hung up, but I thought I'd have time to make it up to her on Christmas Eve."

Every detail came back in sharp relief as he described them to Mia. "The door into the complex used to stick, so it wouldn't close right. I kept meaning to tell the manager. That night it wasn't quite latched shut."

He'd thought nothing of it at the time, nor had he noticed the thin film of blood on the interior knob as he pulled the door shut. "Then I saw the apartment door was open. My first thought was that Elizabeth had gone out and we'd been robbed."

He remembered listening at the door to see if someone was still inside. Later his hesitation had torn him up inside—maybe he could have saved his wife if he'd gone inside those few seconds sooner. Even when the therapist had reminded him Elizabeth had been dead at least an hour by the time he got home, he couldn't let go of the what-ifs.

"I still thought it was a burglary when I saw the living room torn up. Then I went into the kitchen."

A sob caught at his throat. He dragged in breath after breath to keep from breaking down.

"I yelled her name. Screamed it so loud the whole floor heard me. When she wouldn't answer me I grabbed her and shook her."

She'd been so limp. Her blood was everywhere, and he'd gotten it on his hands, his clothes. It hadn't helped his case later, no matter how many times he'd tried to explain it to the police.

For a long time after, he could still feel her blood on his hands, even after he washed them. "I called 9-1-1. The police came and took my statement. Three weeks later, they arrested me."

Mia stirred. "There was a witness."

"A homeless woman picked me out of a lineup. Phillips was my height and build. He'd been wearing gloves, so the only prints were mine."

"What made the police look for him?" Mia asked.

He laughed without humor. "They didn't. Dawson knew I hadn't killed her, so he hired a private investigator to keep digging."

"And he found Reggie Phillips?"

"Thanks to sheer luck. The old guy across the hall from us, Mr. Padresky, had dementia. He'd gotten so paranoid, he'd rigged up a video camera out in the hall, hidden behind a light. Afraid someone was out to get him, I guess."

Elizabeth used to visit the old man, bringing him borscht

and rugelach, listening to him talk about the old country. At the time, Jack hadn't had the patience to listen to Padresky's ravings like Elizabeth did. Now he regretted his indifference.

"Mr. Padresky died a month after Elizabeth was killed. When the P.I. went down to the apartment to question my neighbors, Padresky's son was there cleaning out his father's apartment. The son had found the camera and a stack of video tapes. He gave them to the P.I."

"And Reggie was on one of the tapes."

"He was caught going in and coming out." The police had shown him the tape, hoping he knew the man. The image of Phillips's crazed eyes, Elizabeth's blood splattered on his face, was burned into Jack's mind. "The homeless woman recognized him, knew where he hung out. Phillips still had the gloves."

The ugliness of the past clung to Jack like a shroud, seemed to dim the room despite the brightness of the sun streaming in through the window. With an effort he pulled himself back to the present.

And gazed down at Mia, looking up at him. Her smile, her eyes sent a message that tore away the darkness, poured joy into his well of grief.

He looked away, unprepared, overwhelmed. Eased away from her and rose.

She stood, letting the comforter fall away. Her smile fading, she stared out the bedroom window at the thicket of trees outside. Melted away by the sun, snow no longer frosted the branches of the ponderosas and cedars. A squirrel scolded a jay as it sailed by with a deep-blue flash of wings.

"I know Christmas means too much to you, Jack. That you can never forget. But for today, can it just be Christmas?"

A few days ago it would have seemed impossible. But

with Mia beside him, he thought he might be able to find some joy in the day as he once had. "I have a gift for you."

Surprise flickered across her face and her smile returned. "I have one for you, too."

He couldn't hold back his own smile, couldn't resist kissing her. "Let's open them out in the great room."

Laughing with a child's exuberance, she hurried from the room. Jack stopped to pick up his wedding photo, still on the floor by the foot of the bed.

As he gazed down at Elizabeth's radiant face, he steeled himself for the familiar grief. But like the snow that had lost its grip on the tree branches when the sun warmed it, it seemed Mia had shaken loose his sorrow. He felt a sadness for everything he lost when Elizabeth died, but the emotion lacked the intensity that had so often brought him to his knees.

That in itself was Christmas gift enough from Mia. Even when she left him—he ignored the bone-deep ache he felt contemplating that eventuality—he could think of her, remember how she brought light back into his life.

Setting the photo carefully back on the dresser, he retrieved the wrapped package he'd tucked into the closet. He'd had a hell of a time finding Christmas paper, finally locating the red-and-green-striped roll buried on a shelf in the garage.

Mia was sitting on the sofa, long legs folded under her, the firelight shimmering in her hair. As he stood behind her, out of her field of view, his imagination moved into dangerous territory—sharing his life with Mia, having her with him always. Having again what he'd had with Elizabeth.

Except he didn't love Mia, wouldn't love her. He'd had his world ripped inside out when Elizabeth died. She had been his one and only. His experience with Joanna had shown him that his ability to recognize real love had died with his wife.

It was just as well Mia was temporary. If he loved her he wouldn't be able to let her leave. That he was willing to say goodbye was just further proof that she didn't mean that much to him.

"Are you going to rip that open yourself?" Her question startled him.

He looked down at the package in his hands, realized he gripped it so tightly, his fingers tore holes in the cheery wrapping paper. He forced himself to relax as he moved around the sofa and set the gift in her lap. "Merry Christmas."

She held out a roll of paper tied with a length of purple yarn. "No fancy gift wrap, I'm afraid."

Recognizing the paper as a sheet from her sketch pad, he guessed she'd given him a drawing. He swung onto the sofa beside her. "You go first."

She bent her head to the package, plucking at the curled green ribbon until she untied the knot. Once she'd loosened the ribbon, she carefully ran a thumbnail through each piece of tape to open the package without tearing the red and green paper.

"Elizabeth ripped open her presents like a four-year-old," Jack said, smiling at the memory.

"I want to save the paper," Mia said. "For later."

When she left. He gritted his teeth against that reality, focusing on Mia as she opened her present.

She lifted the hand-loomed cashmere scarf from the box, the firelight enriching the deep emerald-and-royal-blue weave. "It's beautiful."

"I bought it for my sister a few years ago. I'd forgotten she's allergic to wool." He'd wanted to give Mia something that hadn't belonged to Elizabeth. The moment he saw the scarf again, he could picture it nestled around Mia's neck, the rich colors warm against her pale skin.

As if she'd read his mind, she wrapped the soft length of cashmere around her, draping it across her shoulders like a shawl. A vivid image intruded—Mia in the scarf and nothing else, the fringed ends concealing, then revealing her breasts.

"Open yours," she said.

He shook off his erotic fantasy. Taking his time, he undid the bow, then unrolled the paper. Mia watched him, her expression intent.

Jack couldn't hold back his smile when he revealed William's grinning face. "I'm surprised you could get him to sit still long enough to draw him."

"He e-mailed a school photo."

She'd found the one bright spot in his life, had managed to capture it with her skilled hand. He'd have this, at least, to remember her by.

"Thank you," he said, pulling her into his arms.

Her slender body felt so slight against his. She was as evanescent as the snow outside melting in the sun. His for the moment, then quickly gone.

He couldn't keep letting her in like this. If he didn't start shutting her out, the agony when she left would only be that much worse.

Yet even as he told himself that, he still held her, inhaling her scent, listening to her breathe.

Chapter Fourteen

After her latest meltdown and their exchange of gifts, Mia felt even more unsettled. Something frightening loomed in the mists of her mind, momentarily held at bay by the simple joy of Christmas, but waiting for its chance to strike. She knew she had no choice but to face it down, yet she feared the eventual confrontation.

She wanted to talk to Jack about it, feel the comfort of his arms around her. After he'd shared with her what had happened the night his wife died, it seemed the burden that always weighted him down had eased. She'd thought she could even have told him what she'd buried deep inside her—that she loved him. But when he'd come out to the great room with his gift for her, she could see something still lay heavily on his shoulders. It didn't feel right to weigh him down even more with her own problems.

Then the house phone had rung and he took the call in his office. After he'd left, Mia carefully folded the striped wrapping paper. The act seemed so familiar, she assumed it was a habit of hers. Yet another bit of useless information about her past life that her mind had stingily doled out.

The dribs and drabs of personality popping up in her consciousness were too disparate for her to reassemble into her life. Without a picture of herself, there was no way of knowing where the pieces fit or what the puzzle looked like. There had to be a way to reach deeper, to pull out her true self.

Even as the idea popped into her mind, she shrank from it. The scent of cinnamon had a connection to her former life. She didn't understand the link, but it seemed powerful. It had brought out the ugliest of experiences, the most frightening. But maybe if she forced the issue, she might see behind the dark and faceless window into the world in which she belonged.

Unless she took a different path, one more terrifying than rediscovering her past, yet more glorious. If she only had enough courage.

Her hands buried in the ends of the cashmere scarf, she watched Jack's office door as it swung open.

"How's Mrs. Franklin?" Mia asked as Jack walked through the great room.

"She's home, feeling fine." At the stove, he held his hands out to the fire's warmth. "They're heading out to her sister's place for the rest of the day."

"That's good." She stretched out her legs and rose from the sofa. "There's something I want to talk to you about."

He looked back at her over his shoulder, and for a moment, the lightness she'd seen earlier was there in his face again. *Tell him now,* an inner voice whispered. The words clung to her lips, ready to spill out.

But then, like a shutter closing, the lightness was gone. The weight returned. "What about?" he asked, his tone unwelcoming.

Suddenly the house seemed to close in on her. "Could we go out? Walk for a little while?"

He didn't seem happy about that, but he pulled out his parka and boots and the ski overall for her. After directing her to pull on two pairs of socks and the overlarge shoes, he cut up a plastic garbage bag and sealed pieces over Mia's feet with duct tape. The socks would keep her feet warm and the plastic would keep most of the wet out for the short time they'd be in the snow. The scarf around her neck would add another layer of warmth.

After so many days sequestered inside, Mia's spirits rose as they stepped from the house. The brilliant white of the pristine snow took her breath away. It sparkled in the sun's light as if diamonds had been sprinkled on it's surface. The sky was an impossible shade of blue, its cornflower hue contrasting vividly with the dense green of the trees.

They walked out between the cedars and redwoods, following the path Jack had stamped out. Blue jays screamed as they skimmed from tree to tree, like a fragment of sky let loose.

They continued past the last of Jack's footprints, Jack moving slowly as he forged a trail. If she lagged behind, he'd stop and turn back, waiting for her while she caught up, putting out a hand to help her keep her balance. It reminded her of that first walk they'd taken shortly after she'd arrived, and she reflected on how much had happened since then.

They couldn't go as far as they had that day, not with knee-deep snow impeding their progress. With Mia gasping for breath from the exertion, she let Jack pull her up on a stout fallen tree. They sat on the log, shoulders brushing, his gloved hand beside hers on the damp bark.

"Tell me," he said softly.

Forward or back? Which direction should she go? Her mind told her she shouldn't desert the woman she'd once been, but her heart sang a different story.

"What if I don't go back?"

His tension was immediate, his jaw flexing with it and his shoulders taut. "What do you mean?"

He knew what she meant, she could see it in his eyes. But he wasn't giving an inch. She would have to spell it out.

Her throat went dry. "What if I stay here with you?"

She saw it just for an instant—hope flared in his face, as dazzling as the sun-kissed snow. Then he turned away, staring off into the trees. "No."

Her fingers in the thick gloves dug into the tree trunk. "Why not?"

"You have a life out there, Mia. You damn well can't pretend it didn't happen. That it isn't waiting for you."

"Maybe I don't want that life back." *Because I love you!* Except she still couldn't bring herself to say it out loud.

"Whatever you think you want from me, it's not in me to give. Not anymore."

"It doesn't matter." She reached for his hand, forced the words from her throat. "We don't have to love each other."

His gaze locked on to her face, fierce and angry. "Is that what you want? To use each other that way? When I feel that knife in my heart remembering Elizabeth, I should just lose myself in you until I don't feel it anymore?"

He curved his fingers around the back of her neck, sliding beneath the whorls of the scarf. "And I'll be your secret little escape from nightmares. Because you'd rather sleep with a stranger, a man you don't love, than face whatever has you so scared."

He pressed his mouth to hers, all his anger burning through the contact. She pushed against him, and his chest seemed hard and immovable. Fear spurted up inside her, blacking out her vision, speeding her heart to a pounding roar. A scream welled up, pushed at her throat, but it never had a chance to emerge because he'd already let her go, a look of horror on his face.

"Dammit, dammit, dammit!" He pushed off the log, kicking at the snow, slamming a fist into the trunk of a nearby ponderosa. Mia covered her face with her hands, shaking all over.

"Mia." Contrition in his face, he reached a hand out toward her.

She didn't take it. Not because she was afraid of him; her fear had had nothing to do with Jack. But she couldn't ignore her reaction to his brief flare of anger. She realized she wouldn't be able to go forward without first going back. Even if she could convince Jack to accept her into his life, she would have to deal with her fears first.

"There's something I have to do," she told him.

She slid from the log, accepting his hand to steady her as she dropped to the snow. This time she walked ahead of him. When she stumbled once or twice, his hand went to her elbow to right her before she fell.

Back inside the house, she stripped off the ski overall and gloves. She had to push herself to walk into the kitchen, to drag out the step stool. She found the tin of cinnamon sticks, made sure the lid was shut tightly. Then she brought her sketch pad out to the great room.

Jack had spread their outerwear by the fire to dry, and now he stood watching her as she sat cross-legged on the sofa. She looked up at him. "Stay with me. Please."

He moved to the other end of the sofa as she opened the pad to a fresh sheet. With trembling hands she opened the lid of the tin and pulled out a cinnamon stick. She tried to snap it in two, but her hands shook so badly, she couldn't manage it.

"I'll do it," Jack said, reaching across for the slender brown stick.

She jolted at the crack of the cinnamon bark breaking. Then he handed her the pieces and the fragrance filled her nostrils. Her heart hammered in her chest as she shut her eyes.

At first she could only hear the unsteady rasp of her breathing, could see nothing but the orange flicker of firelight through her eyelids. She inhaled deeply, letting the spiciness curl on her tongue, move into her lungs.

The scent grew stronger, sharper. It seemed to blow into her face in irregular puffs. The faint orange of firelight disappeared, replaced by a face looming large and angry over her.

He was shouting at her, the words angry and ugly. His lips and tongue were red, colored by the disk of cinnamon candy on his tongue. Each time he struck her, he said terrible things about her, and she tried to shrink smaller and smaller with each blow.

She knew the monster's face as her father's and the girl he struck was herself, a tiny little thing cowering in the kitchen. But even as he shouted at her, the scene shifted to a different place—a hotel room?—and she transformed from that helpless girl to a grown woman. Now she wore the red Christmas sweater and the jeans she'd worn when she'd arrived here, running shoes on her feet.

But the same man beat her, his eyes filled with rage, the odor of cinnamon clinging to him like a dank smog. Even as his fists rained down on her, his mouth spewing obscenities, his face melted and changed, now her father's, now the monster's. The scene would hitch and restart, again and again, the same blows inflicted in an endless loop.

She lurched out of the flashback with a gasp, hands flailing out to protect herself from the phantoms in her mind. The touch of Jack's fingers on her arm terrified her until she brought herself back to the present.

Her chest heaved as she sucked in a lungful of air. Covering his hand with her own, she held tight to him, fighting to ground herself. With one last squeeze, she let go and picked up her pencil.

Her fingers moved like lightning across the pad, laying down lines and curves, shading between them. A dark streak here, a pale brush of the pencil edge there. She was scarcely aware of what she was drawing, only faintly aware of Jack in the room, turning up the fire as shadows lengthened, throwing the afghan over her as the room grew chilly.

She leaned over the pad as she drew, unwilling to share the sketch until she finished. Jack seemed to understand; he kept his distance, moving through the room without disturbing her.

By the time she drew the last stroke, her hand had cramped so badly she could barely hold the pencil. She dropped the pad facedown on the sofa beside her and tossed the pencil on the end table. Then she stood as close as she could to the pellet stove, desperate for the heat.

Jack came over and wrapped his arms around her, pulling

her into his warmth. One by one the taut muscles within her body relaxed and she almost felt herself again.

"What did you see?" he asked as he stroked her back.

"The same as before, my father beating me." She gulped back her fear. "But then it changed." She told him about the hotel room, how she'd seen her present-day self being beaten.

"Could your father have found you?" Jack asked. "Attacked you?"

"It looks that way. He must have come to my room—maybe in a hotel near here. I let him in…" Tears suddenly clutched at her throat as she realized the magnitude of her mistake. "How could I have let him in? Shouldn't I have known he would do this to me?"

His hand trailed across her back soothingly. "Maybe he told you he was there to make amends. You might have wanted to give him a second chance."

"There are still too many unanswered questions." Frustration filled her. "I don't know my name, who the rest of my family is. And how did I get here to your property?"

"I think you drove. Once we're able to get out of here, we'll find your car down the road."

The reminder of how soon she'd be leaving him sent an ache of longing through her. She wished another storm would hit, a dozen storms, piling up snow so high she would never be able to get out. Force him to let her stay.

"What did you draw?" His question pulled her from her wishful thinking.

"I'm not even sure." She pulled away and picked up the pad, bringing it over to the light of the fire.

She was glad for Jack's nearness, that his arm curved around her shoulder as they stood side by side. She needed his support as she gazed down at the fiend she'd rendered with paper and pencil.

It wasn't a human face. The creature could have escaped from hell, with its fanged mouth, the deformities sprouting from its cheeks and chin. The hair hung in sparse tangles, the nose was nothing more than holes above the thin lips.

Only the eyes looked human, dark and shockingly kind, a travesty in that hideous face. They were familiar, too, although she couldn't quite puzzle out where she'd seen them.

When she recognized them, she went rigid, and Jack's arm dropped from her shoulders. Alarm searing her, she glanced up at him. "They're your eyes," she whispered.

He'd hurt her. He'd terrified her, grabbing her so roughly out there in the snow, almost punishing her with his kiss. With all Mia had been through, to traumatize her further with his actions was inexcusable.

Why else had she drawn his eyes in that monster's face? He felt sick at the thought. He would cut his own hands off rather than touch her in anger again.

The business line rang in his office, giving him a reprieve from his guilt. It had to be Dawson. Other than a wrong number, he'd be the only one to call Jack on Christmas.

"Hey," Dawson said in greeting. "How are you doing?"

"Fine." To his amazement he meant it. He was usually a wreck on Christmas after a week of emotional turmoil.

"You sound good." Dawson sounded as surprised as Jack. "An update on the road-clearing crew. With the weather cooperating, they'll start first thing in the morning. For every day less than a week, they get a bonus. You might even be able to get out by the end of the weekend."

A knot formed in Jack's stomach. "That's good. Thanks."

He returned to the great room. "That was Dawson. We'll be out in three days."

She nodded, her expression grave. "About the drawings. The monster having your eyes."

"I shouldn't have hurt you—"

She put up a hand to stop him. "I drew your eyes in his face because it was the only way I could feel safe. Because I knew you'd keep the monster from hurting me."

She reached for him and he couldn't refuse her. He sat beside her, drawing her into his arms, the balm of her forgiveness washing through him.

Chapter Fifteen

They slept together that night in Jack's bed, making love again, this time in darkness, Jack memorizing every curve and hollow of Mia's body with his fingertips. Afterward he held her until dawn crept into the window, drifting off to sleep with her soft hair brushing his cheek.

Just after nine the next morning, after toast and scrambled eggs, they went out together down the road. They chose to walk rather than take the Suburban, Mia in her makeshift snowboots following in his tracks. They heard the heavy equipment before they saw it on the far side of the rockslide. Jack's stomach sank as it hit home how soon Mia would be leaving.

The crew foreman—Mike something, he couldn't remember the last name—waved from his position down along the curve of the road. Dawson had e-mailed Mike's cell-phone number so Jack could get a status report each day. Apparently, they'd begun plowing the road before the 8:00 a.m. start time. Mike stood behind a chest-high snow berm. As narrow as Jack's road was, the plow must have had to back up nearly to the highway before it could turn around.

He and Mia returned to the house more slowly, his hand behind his back so that Mia's fingers could link loosely with his as she followed him. The incline made it difficult to talk, but he doubted he could have mustered up a conversation anyway. Mia would be leaving in only a few days. What else was there to discuss?

Back in the house he poured himself a mug of coffee, then dumped it in the sink when his stomach rebelled. Mia sat on the sofa, legs curled under her, an unopened paperback on her lap. He went out to the great room and sat with her, pulling her into his arms, her back snug against his chest.

"Before you go…" His stomach contracted again. "Draw me one more picture. Of you."

He was a damn masochist to ask, but there was no way he would take back the request. He felt her nod, then she turned to look up at him. "What if I refuse to leave?"

He shut his eyes against the joy that swelled inside him. "You can't."

She turned completely around to face him. "Why not? People reinvent themselves all the time. Start new lives."

"What about your family?" He struggled to invest conviction in his tone. "You could be married. Have children."

She shook her head. "I don't. I know that much. If there were children, I know I wouldn't forget them. If there was a husband…"

"What about your nightmares?" he asked. "The flashbacks. They won't end just because you've stopped trying to remember.".

"I'll deal with them. With you to protect me."

How could he refuse the gift she was offering him? When it was exactly what he wanted?

Could he risk it? Letting her into his life? Letting himself care about her? The temptation burned inside him as he gazed down at her earnest face.

"Jack," she said, her hand resting against his cheek. "You have to know…" Her voice faltered. "I love you."

His heart felt as if it would explode from his chest in exhilaration. He gathered her close again, emotions blasting around inside him like a hurricane. He was terrified to try to capture and read them.

He said the most honest thing he could. "I don't know if I can love anyone again."

She stiffened in his arms, but only for an instant. She relaxed again, drawing back to gaze up at him. With her kiss she wrapped herself tightly around his heart. How could he ever bear to let her go?

The weekend passed in a blissful blur for Mia. They didn't discuss the possibility of her staying again, but Jack hadn't refused outright, and she felt certain he was coming to accept the idea.

After they made love Friday night, using the last condom, they had to be creative with the lack of protection. She would just as soon have not bothered, would have been thrilled to find herself pregnant with Jack's baby. But he insisted, still holding himself back from the notion of her permanence in his life.

Just as Dawson had predicted, by Sunday night the work crew cleared enough of the rockslide to allow Jack to drive his Suburban down to the highway. Jack was happy to wait until Monday morning to head up to Tahoe. After their Sunday dinner, they worked together on a list of needed supplies. Jack made no mention of a visit to the sheriff's department, and Mia's hopes soared.

It was nearly eight when Jack went into his office to send a quick e-mail to Dawson. Mia had found a Scrabble board squirreled away in the guest-room closet and they planned to play a game once he was finished. As she set up the board on the coffee table, she contemplated an X-rated version of the game and what that might lead to.

When Jack returned a few minutes later, her welcoming smile faded when she saw his shuttered expression. "William's on the Web cam."

Her heart sank, certain the boy wouldn't be contacting Jack at ten o'clock Chicago time if all was well. "Is his mother sick again?"

"You need to come talk to him."

If Mrs. Franklin had had a relapse, William wouldn't want to talk to Mia. A knot drew tight inside her, refusing to release even when she saw the eight-year-old's grinning face on the computer screen.

"I told you I'd remember!" he said exuberantly. "I forgot 'cause it was so long ago—back in May. My friend Eric and me wanted to nominate our teacher, Mrs. Burnett, for an award. We were searching the Web for teacher awards and that's when we found you."

Jack turned to her, his gaze impenetrable. "He sent a link." The URL glowed blue at the bottom of the Web-cam window.

She lowered herself into Jack's chair, her knees suddenly weak. Edging the mouse over the link, she clicked.

She'd barely absorbed the headline, "Local Educator Wins Teaching Award," before her gaze dropped to the photo accompanying the article. She could see only the top of the person's head and had to scroll down to see the face.

She fell back in the chair, her hand dropping to her side. It was her smiling from the screen. Her hair was longer, just past her shoulders, her face fuller and younger, but it was her.

She scrolled back up and read the first line of the four-year-old article. "Goodyear Middle School teacher, Teresa Leoni—"

She couldn't read anymore as recognition of her real name hit her with the force of a slap. Her throat dry, she had to swallow before she could speak. "I'm Teresa Leoni."

"We'd better see what else we can find." He dragged over the other chair and pulled the keyboard toward him. A search of Teresa Leoni brought up dozens of results. When Jack added the word *missing,* it winnowed the hits down to eight.

All of them about her.

The search result included the story headlines. Middle School Teacher Reported Missing. Whereabouts of Eighth-Grade Teacher Still Unknown. Parents at Phoenix-Area School Join Search for Missing Teacher.

She scanned the list, all of them variations on the first three. Until she got to the last item.

Fiancé of Missing Teacher Offers Reward.

She glanced at Jack, knew from the grim set of his mouth, the tension in his hands on the keyboard that he'd read the last headline. He moved the mouse down to the last search result and clicked.

She made to turn away from the computer, but he grabbed the arm of the chair and slid her back into place. He was right to keep her there. She had to look. Had to confront the life she'd been so ready to walk away from.

She didn't want to see the man's face and was grateful when only her own photo illustrated the article. It was more recent than the one from the piece about her teaching award, her face thinner, her haircut even more severe than how she now wore it. Her smile seemed strained and she could see a man's arm around her shoulder. The rest of him had been cropped out of the picture.

She picked his name out of the first paragraph—Robert Hiskins. She felt queasy reading the name, no doubt because she didn't want to think of herself loving anyone but Jack. Otherwise the name drew a blank.

She forced herself to skim the rest, finding the pertinent details. She taught eighth-grade biology and physical science at Goodyear Middle School. She'd taken off for Christmas break a week early so she and her fiancé could have a long vacation driving around California.

After spending the night of December 13 in San Bernardino, the article said, she and Robert had made their way up to a motel in Lake Tahoe. The next night, she'd gone down to the lobby for a soda. Robert said he'd fallen asleep waiting for her and didn't realize she hadn't returned until he woke the next morning. He'd reported her missing on Monday, December 15.

Jack sat beside her, his arms crossed tightly over his chest. "It explains how you got from Goodyear to Tahoe."

"But not how I got here."

"I'm sure your fiancé will clarify that point," Jack said, his voice void of emotion, "when we contact him."

An unreasonable panic filled her. "I don't want to contact him."

"The police will when I take you down to the sheriff's station." All the warmth had left his tone.

"I thought I was staying with you, Jack."

"I never agreed to that." The words struck her heart like sharp stones. "Now that I know about your fiancé—"

"I don't love him! I love you!"

His dark eyes wouldn't meet hers. "You did love him. Two weeks ago, he was the man you wanted to spend the rest of your life with."

"I don't remember him. I don't remember loving him." She took Jack's hand. "Whatever I might have felt before was wiped away when I fell in love with you."

For a moment she thought she'd convinced him. His hand closed around hers, holding it so gently, as if what was most precious in the world to him lay wrapped in his fingers.

But then he let her go, pushing back in the chair and letting her hand fall to her lap. He rose, standing over her, his face impassive.

"Give it time. You'll remember. And I won't mean anything to you anymore."

He walked away. Teresa dropped her head in her hands and wept.

He'd known it would end up this way, hadn't he? That eventually, they would find out who Mia was—Teresa, not Mia—and this interlude between them would end. That the hours in each other's arms would be nothing more than a dream he would relive in the dark hours when despair overcame him.

He could keep her here. Could tell her he changed his

mind, that he wanted her to stay. To hell with the fiancé and their engagement. To hell with the doubts that would spring up in Teresa's mind sooner or later when she wondered if Robert Hiskins really had been the love of her life.

As much as Jack wanted her, as much as he couldn't bear the thought of her leaving, he'd never do that. Because eventually, when it hit her that her decision to stay had been a mistake, it would kill him to see that realization in her eyes.

Standing at his bedroom window, he heard her steps in the hall as they approached his closed door. He imagined her lifting her hand to knock, then hesitating. Was she thinking about her fiancé, wondering about their relationship? Maybe her true feelings for her fiancé had already come back to her, and she wanted Jack to know.

When she did rap on the door, he didn't answer, had to force himself to stay where he was. If she wanted to tell him her memories about Robert had returned, he didn't want to hear it. If she was knocking on his door to ask him again if she could stay, he couldn't let her speak the words. Because he wasn't sure he could say no again.

When he didn't answer, she tried the door. He'd locked it, not trusting himself to resist her if she entered his room. When he and Mia—*Teresa*—had made love, he hadn't known he was sleeping with another man's fiancée. He couldn't ignore the knowledge now, never mind what his body was screaming at him to do.

She called through the door, his name on her lips like a punch to the chest. He gritted his teeth to keep quiet. Counted his breaths, listened to the dull thud of his heart, stared out into the blackness of the snow-covered night. Anything to bear the waiting until she walked away.

After what seemed an eternity, he heard her footfalls again, fading as she returned back down the hall. He could just make out the sound of her bedroom door shutting.

His shoulders still knotted with tension, he crossed to the bed, grabbing the portable as he sank onto the edge. His first call was to Dawson. Jack's friend had connections who could suss out any phone number. It was nearly 9:00 p.m. on a Sunday, but Jack knew Dawson would deliver.

An hour later the phone rang, Dawson's home number on the caller ID. If he wondered about Jack's request, Dawson didn't let on as he read off the number.

The slip of paper with Hiskin's number seemed to burn Jack's hand as he paced down the hall to Teresa's room. Through her open door, he saw her on the bed, the sketch pad in her lap.

He stood in the doorway. "I'm calling him."

She didn't ask who. "You found his phone number?"

"Dawson did. Would you rather fly there or have him come here?"

"You know what I want."

He wanted it, too, but that didn't make it right. "I'll make the arrangements."

She nodded acquiescence. He returned to his room, wanting to drop the scrap of paper into the fire, let it burn to ashes. Instead he picked up the phone.

It would be almost 11:00 p.m. in Goodyear, but if Hiskins was any kind of man at all, he would welcome the late call if it meant good news about his fiancée. It crossed Jack's mind that he ought to notify the Goodyear Police Department or even the El Dorado County Sheriff. But Jack knew if it was him, he'd want to know about Teresa's safety ASAP. His jaw aching, Jack stabbed out the number.

Hiskins answered on the second ring. "Hello?"

Just hearing his voice, Jack hated the man, but he pushed himself to speak. "My name is Jack Traynor." He dragged in a breath. "I found your fiancée."

The silence stretched so long, Jack thought he'd lost the connection. "Mr. Hiskins?"

"You found Teresa? Where?" He sounded cautious, not jubilant. Maybe he'd fielded dozens of calls from crackpots and didn't want to get his hopes up.

"Near my house. About twenty miles west of South Lake Tahoe."

Another long silence, then, "How do you know it's her?" Still that guarded tone, as if he didn't want to give away too much. With the ten-thousand-dollar reward he'd offered, Jack supposed the man had to be careful.

The article had mentioned what Teresa had been wearing—describing the Christmas sweater and jeans in detail. But there was one item that had been omitted from the reports. "She was wearing an ankle bracelet with Mia written in gold."

"Oh." He seemed to choke on the word. "When was this?"

"On the forteenth. I found her walking across my property. She nearly drowned—"

"W-walking?" The man's voice faltered. "Teresa is alive?"

"She's been through some kind of trauma. Couldn't remember who she was or anything about her life. She's been staying with me—"

"She couldn't remember how she got there?" Now Jack could hear the excitement in Hiskins's tone. "What about what happened before?"

"She doesn't remember any of it." She doesn't remember *you,* Jack wanted to say, but he held his tongue. "We're won-

dering if it had something to do with her father. He was abusive
when she was a child…could he have attacked her again?"

Hiskins considered the question for a long moment.
"Maybe."

"Could he have known about your trip to Tahoe? Maybe
he'd called Teresa that night, asked her to meet him?"

"Sure," Hiskins said, although he sounded anything but.

What did it matter? Hiskins was Teresa's fiancé and soon
enough, she'd be in his arms. It would be his job to protect
her from her father.

They finished the call, working out the details of how
Hiskins and Teresa would be reunited. Hiskins had wanted
Jack to put Teresa on the first available plane to Phoenix, but
Jack used the excuse of Teresa's still-fragile physical state to
insist Hiskins fly to Sacramento. Jack gave the man his e-mail
so Hiskins could forward his flight information to Jack once
he'd made the reservation.

Plans made, Jack hung up and dropped the phone back into
the charger. He knew damn well it was for his own benefit
he'd wanted Hiskins to fly here rather than the other way
around. Jack wanted more time with Teresa.

And that time would start now. He couldn't make love to
her again, wouldn't trespass on another man's territory that
way. But if he was going to be without her for the rest of his
life, maybe he could fill the emptiness of his heart with her
nearness to make the stark loneliness easier to bear later.

He returned to her room where she was still holding the
art pad. A hand mirror from the bathroom sat beside her.

She turned the pad toward him as he approached the bed. His
heart squeezed so tight he thought it would never beat again.

Her face, sketched in pencil, gazed up at him from the page.

Her expression was grave, but he didn't need a smile to see the clear message in the perfectly drawn eyes.

She loved him. As powerfully as Elizabeth had. In a way that would heal him forever.

But he would have to send her back to her fiancé. Because as genuine as that love might be, it was misplaced. When she saw Robert Hiskins again, her emotions would shift back to him.

Taking the pad from her hands, Jack set it aside and laid on the bed. Fully dressed, he pulled her into his arms.

He stayed awake as long as he could. Watched the clock ticking off the hours until well after 3:00 a.m. When he finally slept, his dreams were full of her and his every secret wish was fulfilled. She loved him and she was his forever.

Chapter Sixteen

Teresa woke to the sound of heavy machinery nearby. She could still feel Jack's warmth on the sheets and pillowcase, so he must have just left the bed. She was loath to move, to give up this last vestige of his heat.

He returned before she'd pushed back the covers, and sat beside her on the bed. "The snowplow driver came back to clear the road up to the house."

Which meant there was nothing to keep them from leaving. "What time was his plane coming in?"

She couldn't bring herself to speak Robert's name. The man felt like a complete stranger to her, the way Jack had when she'd first woken in front of his fire. Except now Jack's was the familiar face. She couldn't even picture what Robert looked like.

"I just downloaded his e-mail. He'll be arriving in Sacramento around eleven. I told him we'd meet him at the airport."

She felt queasy at the thought. "What if I don't recognize him?"

"Once you see him—"

"I can't remember anything about him." Panic surged up inside her. "How can I go back to Arizona with him if I don't know him?"

"Let's just take it a step at a time." He rose, moving away from the bed. "It's an hour and a half from here to the airport. I thought we'd head down the hill early, get breakfast in Placerville."

"It's barely past eight. I'd rather stay here, with you."

His arms crossed over his chest, his gaze fixed on her still warm in the bed. "That's not a good idea, Teresa."

Her real name on his lips stroked her like a caress. She wanted to hear it again and again, whispered in her ear as he kissed her. Made love to her one last time.

He turned toward the door. "I want to get on the road in half an hour." He closed the door behind him.

Her heart heavy, Teresa pushed back the covers. In Elizabeth's pajamas, she gathered up her jeans and one of the hand-me-down sweatshirts. The Christmas sweater had been laundered since she wore it last, but the thought of wearing it hurt. It represented her old life, the one she no longer welcomed reentering.

Showered and dressed, with the sweater and the sketch pad in a plastic market bag, she joined Jack in the great room. She'd left the drawing of her on the bed, a promise kept.

Jack pulled on his parka. "Do you have the ankle bracelet?"

She'd forgotten it entirely, hadn't looked at it since that day she'd hidden it in the bathroom drawer. "I don't want it."

As they wended their way down Jack's road, she stared out

the window, biting her lip to keep from crying. She half hoped the rockslide would give way again, blocking their path to the highway. But the crew Dawson had hired had done their job well, reinforcing the mountainside against a repeat rock fall.

They stopped for breakfast in the town of Placerville, El Dorado's county seat. She picked at the waffle she'd ordered, finally pushing it away. Jack didn't do much better with his ham-and-cheese omelet, eating less than half of it.

They climbed back in the car and continued down the road. The pine trees of the higher elevations gave way to oaks and rolling grassland, and grief weighed more and more heavily on Teresa's shoulders.

They pulled into the airport parking structure at ten-thirty. After he turned off the engine of the Suburban, Jack looked at her, and in the dimness she met his gaze, drinking in his beloved face. She saw the naked need he'd tried to hide and something else she doubted he would ever admit. Not when another man would soon be touching down to claim her.

She jolted with a sudden realization. "Why was I wearing a bracelet with another woman's name?"

Jack's brow furrowed as he considered her question. "Your mother's name?"

"My mother's name is Louise." Then another tantalizing bit of trivia popped into her consciousness. "Mia is Italian for '*mine*.'"

The realization made her uneasy. Had her fiancé given her the bracelet? Branded her as his? When Jack climbed from the Suburban, her heart picked up its pace. She couldn't bring herself to open her door, and waited for Jack to come around to do it.

As they stood just outside the terminal's security check-point, her tension wound up even tighter. She gripped Jack's hand, praying that the flight would be late, that it would be canceled. That Robert would call Jack's cell to say he wouldn't be coming after all. But the nearby displays told her the plane was on time.

At a quarter after eleven, the foot traffic exiting the secure area thickened. Teresa huddled even closer to Jack, watching the faces of every man striding toward them, terror overwhelming her. When they walked past her without recognition, she felt a brief relief before the next man approached.

Then a man with blue eyes, curly blond hair and a ready smile emerged from the crowd. Spotting her with Jack, he hurried toward them. Just as she'd feared, she didn't know him, and when he grabbed her away from Jack to hug her, she nearly screamed. Only a sharp breath in kept the horror from spilling out.

Then the stench of cinnamon hit her, rolling in waves off Robert as he held her close. With the rank smell, the memories crashed into her mind—fists punching, feet kicking, a snarl of rage spewing obscenities. Her begging for mercy as Robert struck her over and over.

Now she did scream, twisting out of his arms and flinging herself toward Jack's safety. "I remember," she gasped out. "It was him. Robert's the one who beat me."

She glanced up at Jack, saw the murderous look on his face. She heard running footsteps and looked over her shoulder to see Robert dashing away—up the walkway, back toward the gates and into the secure area. The TSA agent shouted at him to stop, but Robert kept running. Two other agents joined the chase, surrounding Robert and restraining him. "Sweetheart, baby," Jack murmured as her shaking body all but fell apart. "It's okay. You're safe."

Beyond them, airport security had escorted Robert to a table in the security checkpoint. "I remember everything now. I have to talk to them, tell them what he did."

He held her close, his breathing soothing her. "I want you to know—I would have followed you. I would have been on the next plane to Phoenix."

"To make sure I was okay?" she asked, not wanting to hope for too much.

"To make sure you loved him."

"I don't. I might have once, but after what he did to me, it killed any chance I could love him again."

She could feel Jack's relief as the tension left his body. "Then I have to tell you…" His arms tightened around her. "I love you, Teresa. With all my heart. I want you to be with me forever."

Joy burst inside her at his admission. She reached up to cradle his face in her hands. "And I love you, so very, very much."

He kissed her then, and she could feel his deep love for her with that silent contact. She reveled in the miracle he'd given her—her old life back and a new one just as precious.

Epilogue

It wasn't a white Christmas at her parents' home in San Antonio, but her first holiday as Mrs. Jack Traynor was a joyful one nonetheless. Her family was a small one—just her mother, Louise, and stepfather, Harold, an aunt and uncle and two young cousins. No sisters or brothers. Her father, the dreaded monster of her nightmares, had died ten years ago in prison.

It had been a year of healing for both her and Jack. She'd recovered nearly all of her old life, remembering family and friends, her favorite students. She'd returned to Goodyear long enough to allow the school district to find a long-term substitute. During that time she'd said her goodbyes and packed up her house. Two weeks later, she moved in with Jack.

Although it hadn't happened overnight, Jack had at last come to terms with his wife's murder. By the time of their summer wedding, he could enjoy sharing his memories of

Elizabeth, could laugh about her crazy sense of humor. He'd told Teresa more than once how much Elizabeth would have enjoyed meeting her.

It had been difficult for Teresa to allow back into her mind what had happened with Robert. He'd been the reason she'd become estranged from her parents. After spending half a dozen years with an abuser herself, her mother had sensed something wrong with Robert, but Teresa had refused to see.

Robert had changed so gradually, attentiveness becoming obsessive control until every aspect of her life was under his thumb. From what she wore to what and how much she ate to how short her hair should be all became part of Robert's domain. And as that control increased, Teresa couldn't see that it was tipping over into the danger zone.

When he finally exploded that night in Tahoe, beating her unconscious, she never saw it coming. When she woke up in Jack's house, she retreated behind the same walls she'd used to protect herself when her father hit her. Except this time the walls were absolute, blocking everything from her conscious mind.

Once she told the police what had happened with Robert, they put together the rest of the details—that he'd panicked, fearing he'd beaten her so badly she was dying and that he had to get rid of her body. It was sheer luck that he'd dumped her so close to Jack's road and that Jack came along when he did.

It took her mother to explain why cinnamon had triggered her memories. Her father had had a fondness for cinnamon candy, using it to mask the smell of alcohol on his breath. Teresa had come to associate the scent with her father's fists. Robert's spicy aftershave had cemented that mental connection.

But that was all safely behind her. Now it was Christmas again, and Teresa sat curled up on her mother's sofa, watching

Jack playing Chutes and Ladders on the floor with her two cousins, eight-year-old Mason and six-year-old Natalie. She could swear he was enjoying the game more than the kids.

Stripping off her apron, her mother sat beside her. "I remember when I gave you that sweater."

Teresa smiled, smoothing a hand over the red sweater with its cheery snowman. "The Christmas before I met Robert."

Her mother gave her a worried look. "I hope you're not still thinking of him. You ate so little at dinner."

Her hand on her belly, Teresa caught Jack's eye. He raised a brow, nodding toward her mother.

Teresa took her mother's hand. "Sorry, Mom. I've just been feeling a little queasy."

Her mother's worried look faded, replaced by a look of sheer bliss. "I'm going to be a grandma."

She nodded, hugging her mother tight, then relinquishing her to Jack. While her mom hurried off to the kitchen to tell her younger sister the news, Jack took Teresa in his arms, settling on the sofa with her.

"Have I told you today how much I love you?" he murmured in her ear.

"At least a dozen times," she responded, laughing. "But you haven't reached your quota yet."

"I love you, Teresa Traynor. With all my heart, all my soul."

"And I love you, Jack Traynor."

She kissed him, reveling in his love, in the miracle of their life together.

* * * * *

THOROUGHBRED LEGACY
*The stakes are high when it comes to love,
horse racing, family secrets
and broken promises.*

*A new exciting Harlequin continuity series coming soon!
Led by New York Times bestselling author Elizabeth Bevarly
FLIRTING WITH TROUBLE*

Here's a preview!

THE DOOR CLOSED behind them, throwing them into darkness and leaving them utterly alone. And the next thing Daniel knew, he heard himself saying, "Marnie, I'm sorry about the way things turned out in Del Mar."

She said nothing at first, only strode across the room and stared out the window beside him. Although he couldn't see her well in the darkness—he still hadn't switched on a light...but then, neither had she—he imagined her expression was a little preoccupied, a little anxious, a little confused.

Finally, very softly, she said, "Are you?"

He nodded, then, worried she wouldn't be able to see the gesture, added, "Yeah. I am. I should have said goodbye to you."

"Yes, you should have."

Actually, he thought, there were a lot of things he should have done in Del Mar. He'd had *a lot* riding on the Pacific Classic, and even more on his entry, Little Joe, but after meeting Marnie, the Pacific Classic had been the last thing on Daniel's mind. His loss at Del Mar had pretty much ended his career before it had even begun, and he'd had to start all over again, rebuilding from nothing.

He simply had not then and did not now have room in his life for a woman as potent as Marnie Roberts. He was a horseman first and foremost. From the time he was a schoolboy, he'd known what he wanted to do with his life—be the best possible trainer he could be.

He had to make sure Marnie understood—and he understood, too—why things had ended the way they had eight years ago. He just wished he could find the words to do that. Hell, he wished he could find the *thoughts* to do that.

"You made me forget things, Marnie, things that I really needed to remember. And that scared the hell out of me. Little Joe should have won the Classic. He was by far the best horse entered in that race. But I didn't give him the attention he needed and deserved that week, because all I could think about was you. Hell, when I woke up that morning all I wanted to do was lie there and look at you, and then wake you up and make love to you again. If I hadn't left when I did— the way I did—I might still be lying there in that bed with you, thinking about nothing else."

"And would that be so terrible?" she asked.

"Of course not," he told her. "But that wasn't why I was in Del Mar," he repeated. "I was in Del Mar to win a race. That was my job. And my work was the most important thing to me."

She said nothing for a moment, only studied his face in the darkness as if looking for the answer to a very important question. Finally she asked, "And what's the most important thing to you now, Daniel?"

Wasn't the answer to that obvious? "My work," he answered automatically.

She nodded slowly. "Of course," she said softly. "That is, after all, what you do best."

Her comment, too, puzzled him. She made it sound as if being good at what he did was a bad thing.

She bit her lip thoughtfully, her eyes fixed on his, glimmering in the scant moonlight that was filtering through the window. And damned if Daniel didn't find himself wanting to pull her into his arms and kiss her. But as much as it might have felt as if no time had passed since Del Mar, there were eight years between now and then. And eight years was a long time in the best of circumstances. For Daniel and Marnie, it was virtually a lifetime.

So Daniel turned and started for the door, then halted. He couldn't just walk away and leave things as they were, unsettled. He'd done that eight years ago and regretted it.

"It *was* good to see you again, Marnie," he said softly. And since he was being honest, he added, "I hope we see each other again."

She didn't say anything in response, only stood silhouetted against the window with her arms wrapped around her in a way that made him wonder whether she was doing it because she was cold, or if she just needed something—someone—to hold on to. In either case, Daniel understood. There was an emptiness clinging to him that he suspected would be there for a long time.

* * * * *

THOROUGHBRED LEGACY
coming soon wherever books are sold!

Thoroughbred *Legacy*

Launching in June 2008

**A dramatic new 12-book continuity
that embodies the American Dream.**

Meet the Prestons, owners of Quest Stables, a successful
horse-racing and breeding empire. But the lives, loves
and reputations of this hardworking family are put at risk
when a breeding scandal unfolds.

Flirting with Trouble

by *New York Times* bestselling author

ELIZABETH BEVARLY

Eight years ago, publicist Marnie Roberts spent seven days
of bliss with Australian horse trainer Daniel Whittleson.
But just as quickly, he disappeared. Now Marnie is
heading to Australia to finally confront the man
she's never been able to forget.

*The stakes are high when it comes to love, horse racing,
family secrets and broken promises.*

A new exciting Harlequin continuity series coming soon!

Cole's Red-Hot Pursuit

Cole Westmoreland is a man who gets what he wants. And he wants independent and sultry Patrina Forman! She resists him—until a Montana blizzard traps them together. For three delicious nights, Cole indulges Patrina with his brand of seduction. When the sun comes out, Cole and Patrina are left to wonder—will this be the end of the passion that storms between them?

Look for

COLE'S RED-HOT PURSUIT

by USA TODAY bestselling author

BRENDA JACKSON

Available in June 2008 wherever you buy books.

Always Powerful, Passionate and Provocative.

HARLEQUIN
More Than Words

"Changing the world, one baby at a time."

—**Sally Hanna-Schaefer,** real-life heroine

Sally Hanna-Schaefer is a Harlequin More Than Words
*award winner and the founder of **Mother/Child Residential Program.***

Discover your inner heroine!

REQUEST YOUR FREE BOOKS!

2 FREE NOVELS PLUS 2 FREE GIFTS!

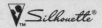

SPECIAL EDITION®

Life, Love and Family!

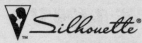

SSECNM0508